Nugent
AR: 7.0

Island of the Loons

Island of the Loons

DAYTON O. HYDE

ATHENEUM   1985   NEW YORK

Library of Congress Cataloging in Publication Data

Hyde, Dayton O.,
    Island of the loons.

    Summary: During the year he is held prisoner by an
escaped convict on an uninhabited island in Lake Superior,
a young boy watches his captor change from desperate
criminal to a gentler man absorbed in the abundant
wildlife of the island.
    [1. Survival—Fiction. 2. Prisoners—Fiction.
3. Islands—Fiction. 4. Animals—Fiction] I. Title.
PZ7.H9676Is 1984   [Fic]   84-2986
ISBN 0-689-31047-1

Published simultaneously in Canada by
McClelland & Stewart, Ltd.
Composition by Westchester Book Composition, Inc.
Yorktown Heights, New York
Printed and bound by Fairfield Graphics
Fairfield, Pennsylvania
Designed by Christine Kettner
First Printing July 1984
Second Printing February 1985

To my brother,
John Livingston Hyde,
who first showed me the island

ACKNOWLEDGEMENTS

My appreciation to Royse and Marge Ellis, who flew me to Island of the Loons, in their Lake Amphibian, and hosted me; Paul Brown, the noted Massachusetts botanist, who made a botanical study of the area; Mary Anne Wyatt and Jocelyn Arundel who worked hard to save the island; and Spencer Beebe, International Director, The Nature Conservancy, whose ideas and contacts eventually made the difference. In addition, I must mention Bert Hopkins, who took me by launch to Caribou Light, and his wife Pearl, who made me welcome. Last but not least, Julia Tibbetts, of Onota, whose heart is as big as the North, who checked my childhood memories for imperfections.

Island of the Loons

one

IF YOU LIVE WITHIN a few hundred miles of Lake Superior, you might recall reading a newspaper account regarding the disappearance of a fourteen-year-old boy nicknamed Jimmy "Munising," who took his battered old lapstrake fishing tug out trolling on the big lake on the first of July and never returned. Rumor had it a tourist saw the boat nodding and bumping along the rocky cliffs east of Munising, but it was soon hidden beyond a point of rocks, and the tourist himself was lost in a stream of vacationers before he could be questioned by authorities.

The loss shook up the town, at least those who assumed that he had drowned, for Jimmy was more than just a local orphan everyone happened to love; he was a special bit of radiance in a northern Michigan lakeside town.

Of course there were many of his fans who suspected the whole matter was just another of Jimmy's pranks, and that tired of playing Huck Finn in some cavern along the shore, he'd show up. Jimmy had a way of showing up.

"On Thursday!" said Mrs. Derleth, refusing to be sad. "On Thursday, never fail, 'cause he knows that's when I bake bread. And, oh! can't he pack it away!"

"That Jimmy Munising," snapped Mrs. Haskall, a few uncertain tears welling under her spectacles. "Just let me wax my floors, and he'll come bounding in the front door packing a shoveful of beach sand in each sole of his Nikes!"

"Sunday, there he'll be," declared Kitty Lennan, as she secured the vines of her scarlet runner beans against the back fence. "All hands and feet and appetite. Just in time for roast beef, smashed potaties 'n peas. But he's some charmer, eh?"

Perhaps Honest Risku, the Alger County Sheriff, might have spent some time searching the coast in his patrol boat had not the Michigan State Police radioed on July 3 that an inmate of the prison farm at Mangum had scaled the chain link fence to vanish in the alder thickets and cedar swamps. A cat burglar or second-story man named Riggs Burkey, he had no experience in the woods and might show up at somebody's farm or a country store, looking for food.

"Wherever that confounded Jimmy is, he'll have to wait," the sheriff muttered, wincing at the wind-flung spume as white-maned waves crashed over the breakwater.

"I got roadblocks to set up, 'n 'sides that, small craft warnings are up, an' I ain't about to give Lake

Superior a chance at adding my name to her long list of victims. She's dangerous enough on a flat calm."

The sheriff drove his patrol car from the docks to the general store, double parked, then, head low, pounded through pelting rain to the planked, covered porch of the ancient building.

"Horus," he called, enjoying a bit of drama as he rushed in the door. "You got any more o' them three-fifty-seven magnum shells—the kind that can shoot through an automobile block. I'm fresh out."

He hopped awkwardly over a pile of dirt just as Horus Matson, the storekeeper, broomed it into the wind. The old man was doing his own sweeping for the first time in years.

"Never let you down before, eh?" the sheriff ventured, lured across the room by the hot barrel stove.

The storekeeper allowed his question to hang in the air as he hung his push broom on a couple of wooden pegs.

"Never," Horus replied. "Not that Jimmy. He had to scramble to make payments on that fish tug." He glanced at the sheriff with the vague disapproval he held for a man who'd lived in Munising twenty years but had been born in Escanaba.

"Think he's playin' tricks? Hid out somewhere, lettin' us worry?"

"Nope. Not this time. Gave me his word he'd be here. True, he did have a sense of humor, well enough, 'n if he saw something funny in hiding out, like getting you off your big butt, he'd sure do it."

The storekeeper slid one thigh up on the counter and sat there swinging his leg. "Full of beans like his mother, Alyce. Now she was a case. Bore three daughters like clockwork, two years apart 'n named every danged one of them Alyce after her. Jimmy hadn't come along a boy, she'd a named him Alyce too."

Horus Matson tossed the sheriff a bag of gumdrops. "On the house," he said as though knowing full well the sheriff was going to help himself anyway.

"A legal secretary, she was," Horus went on. "Smart as a whip. Reckon she'd read as much law as some of them lawyer fellers she worked for. Nobody but Alyce knowed the dad. Kids was all redheaded as a maple tree in autumn, 'n, every time a red-haired stranger showed up in town we'd all holler, 'Alyce! He's here!' We guessed it was some lawyer from somewhere, but nobody knew for sure.

"'Got the kids from a Monkey Ward's catalogue,' Alyce'd say with a grin. 'You won't catch me playing nursemaid to some lazy man!'"

Horus Matson moseyed over to the sporting goods section and slid a box of magnum shells from the shelf, dusting the box with his apron. "Well, poor soul, she died taking her secret with her. The girls, Alyce Marie, Alyce Ruth, and Alyce Anne moved down state where Alyce Marie got a job; but Jimmy, who was two years younger than Alyce Anne, raised such a ruckus they let him stay on, roomin' with Mrs. Haskall. Bought that old beat-up fishing tug when he was only twelve 'n' worked a dozen jobs around town to make the payments. Independent, just like his mother."

The storekeeper set the box of shells on the counter and handed the sheriff a slip to sign. "Reckon if something has happened, we'll miss that kid. Hell, you know this whole town is nuts about Jimmy. One family try to adopt him away from the rest of us there'd be the devil to pay. That kid is all ours boy.

"His mother used the last name, 'Hiram,' but we took to calling him 'Jimmy Munising,' after the town, and the name stuck."

A blast of wind off Lake Superior shook the old store to its foundations and rattled the enamelware on display along the walls.

"Some storm," the sheriff said. "Must be those Roosians testing bombs. You'd a told me we'd have a cold easterly like this in July, I'd a called ya a liar fer sure." He looked about him as though calculating just how much longer the walls could take the wind without collapsing, but in reality bored by a story he knew by heart.

"Got to git," the sheriff put in. "'Nother convict went over the fence at the prison farm. Bugs'll make short work of him. State Police want me to set up a road block, though I dunno why they think he'd be dumb enough to try my bailiwick, what with my rep."

He paused at the door, soaking up one last bit of warmth, one huge hand engulfing the worn brass door latch.

"Last time I saw him," he said wistfully. "Last

time I saw Jimmy, he 'bout run me over with his bike. Red hair flyin' he give me a smile like a cat eating fishbones. When he was headed for that fishing tug of his, a body didn't want to stand in his way."

two

AS THE LAST LOADS OF TACONITE, pellets of partially processed ore, rattled like spent gray musket balls down through the bellies of gondola cars and on through to the cargo holds of the iron ore carrier, the *Charles H. Schaffer,* a diesel locomotive moved along the overhead rails, towing a string of empties back toward the mines in Ishpeming.

Searchlights ablaze, its captain disdaining the help of tugboats, the giant ship slid away from the towering concrete loading dock and slipped on past the wave-battered granite of the breakwater into the stormy darkness of Lake Superior.

Braving the rain in yellow slickers, a team of Michigan State troopers probed the creeping gondolas with searchlight beams. A young corporal leaped for the side of the locomotive and clung there by the grips as the engineer in gray striped cap leaned out the open window.

"Honest, Officer," he said with a grin. "I was only going fifty-five."

The corporal smiled. He was used to taking lip from "Pork" Rose. An old steam engine hogger, Pork, years back, had been picked by L.S. & I. management to try out the first diesel locomotive on the line and only yesterday had soundly beaten the corporal in the finals of a cribbage tournament.

"Honest, Pork, you gave me quite a start!" the corporal called above the rumble of the wheels. "We're looking for a walkaway from the prison farm, and danged if you ain't ugly enough to be him."

"If I see him," Pork called down, "I'll invite him up in the cab for a game or two. Bound to be a better crib player than you are." The old engineer glanced on up the track, then back at the corporal. "Seriously, what you want me to do, eh? Stop the train, or pull on out for Ishpeming?"

"Move her on slow, Pork, so we can have a good look at the cars," the corporal called as he dropped back down on the cinders. "You see your wife, Irene, you give her my best, OK?"

As the caboose disappeared into the night, the corporal moved to his squad car. "Well he's not on the train, at least," he muttered to himself. He leaned in through the open window to grab his mike. "Unit One to K-Niners. OK, Dog Men, trot 'em out!"

From the back of a panel wagon, two long-eared hounds leaped to the ground, then stopped, foreheads wrinkling against the onslaught of the rain as though there were some mistake. Then, knuckling in to commands, each towed its handler back and forth

10

over the area. Sniffing along the track, one dog slowed then pitched ahead, wagging his tail with interest. Moments later, however, it lost enthusiasm, glancing back at its master as though in apology.

"Damn! Looked for a second he was on that con's trail!" the man on the leash shouted. "The corporal's crazy he thinks dogs stand a chance of working in this rain."

A hard volley of sleet caromed off their hats, and violent gusts slammed men and dogs against concrete.

"Must be better ways to make a living," the second handler muttered, shaking with cold, clutching a lightpost to avoid being hurtled into the lake. "Ain't spent one Fourth of July with my family since I got transferred north."

The storm worsened. Waves leaped up the concrete bulwarks like snarling wolves intent on bringing them down.

"Over there!" the first handler yelled above the wind. "Lets try that drier area over there where the cars were standing."

No sooner had the two hounds checked out the new area for scent of their quarry than they scrambled forward, dragging the men forward along the rails.

"Right on!" the lead man called. The hounds went on trailing until the scent vanished, and noses to the concrete they could only mill about.

"K-Nine to Unit One."

"Come in, K-Nine."

"He's been here, Corporal! We're at the end of the dock though and the dogs need wings to go any further. Come in, Unit One. Over."

"Unit One to K-Nine. Stick to your last positive scent until contacted. Ten Four."

There was the sound of running feet, boots slamming against steel and concrete. Guns drawn, the two handlers lay flat against the dock until searchlights, probing, turned night into day, and they picked out other troopers swarming the dock structure like rats in the rafters of a barn. Beams destroyed every shadow, lit up the huge, empty storage bins. No sign of the convict.

"Drury to Unit One."

"Unit One. Come in, Drury."

"Zilch, Corporal. No sign. If he fell down one of these ore hoppers, he's mebbe in bad shape. But alive or dead, he's got to be on that ore boat on his way to Sault Ste. Marie. Over."

"Unit One to Drury. I read you. Get your men back off the dock before someone blows away. We'll have an army waiting at the Sault; the man doesn't have a prayer. Unit One. Ten Four."

One by one, the men came down off the huge dock, checked in with the corporal, and returned in pairs to their squad cars. One by one the huge searchlights blinked out and were towed away until only a few resident safety lights outlined the far reaches and extremities of the structure. As far as the folks of Marquette were concerned, they could sleep easy. The bird had flown; but the cold, icy waters of Lake

Superior would imprison the convict more surely than walls or chains. Once the ore carrier entered the locks at Sault Ste. Marie, a horde of police would be waiting.

three

THE POLICE WERE DEAD RIGHT. Their quarry, Riggs Burkey, was on that boat. He had hitched a ride with a couple of teen-aged boys in a '56 Ford, ridden in style from Mangum right past the prison gates to Marquette, and had been dropped off at the beach not far from the dock. The kids had seemed too spaced out to notice his prison blues, but they had watched their passenger move off toward the iron ore loading facility, then laid a patch for the nearest telephone.

Looking down from his vantage point high atop the ore dock jutting out into Lake Superior, the convict had caught the flash of lights like bright jewels in the dusk as patrol cars sped along the waterfront. He cursed under his breath. The kids had ratted on him. More police cars coming behind the first phalanx. He had picked the coming holiday for his escape attempt because he figured what with the campaign against drunken drivers, the cops would be spread pretty thin.

14

Directly beneath him, a huge tonnage of iron ore pellets slid thundering down into a hold. The man waited for the last pellet to rattle against the steel walls, then jumped blindly into darkness, bouncing hard off a strut as he fell. He lit on his hands and knees, scrambling hard lest more pellets fall and smother him. Clouds of dust choked him. High above he saw lights and braced himself for another dump, but to his relief, an electrically powered set of cranes on rails slammed a heavy hatch cover down on the hold's coaming and all was darkness.

Clad only in thin dungarees, he shivered against the cold, and buried himself up to his chin in taconite, leaving only a small hollow beside his body to allow his hand to reach the pistol strapped beneath his shirt.

Riggs Burkey. Prison Number 390507. Stenciled inside his collar and on his shirt tail. Sentenced 1975. Burglary. A liquor store in Detroit. Of his forty years, seventeen had been spent behind bars. Five feet eleven, black-haired, heavy-faced but narrow-eyed. Complexion pasty. So thick in the shoulders he had to angle sideways to get through a standard door. Eyes like dirty gray smoke. Tore the bicep out of his opponent's arm in a prison grudge fight. After that, the other cons left him in his preferred condition: alone. Illiterate and refused schooling. Prison hobby: wood carving. When it was his pleasure, he could be artistic and especially handy with his hands. His carvings brought a good price in the prison store.

Now he was back in a different kind of prison.

Trapped in Number Three Hold, on an iron ore carrier, outward bound through stormy darkness across the largest fresh water ocean on the planet.

The blackness was absolute, and the cold, seeping through the pellets, made his rain-drenched garb worse than nothing. But his long years of confinement helped him. No need to panic. He was simply in another solitary cell, biding his time, awaiting another chance to escape.

In the distance, he heard the thunder of pellets dropping into holds down the line, and he could feel the ship settle into the water as holds filled and hatch covers thumped against waterproof gaskets. The owners would crowd in every ton they could, right up to and maybe a little beyond legal freeboard.

The ship shuddered through its very bowels and ceased to slam against the pier; engines roared, and through steel plates he could hear the slap of heavy chop, feel the giant carrier strain and roll with its burden as it turned away from the dock into Lake Superior. The vibration seemed to settle the pellets about his body and started a minor avalanche somewhere in the darkness above, loosing streams of taconite, which hammered against his face and swept on past on either side.

Seeking warmth, he worked deeper into the pellets. He remembered as a child he'd once made up a poem. The neighbor kids giggled and pointed their fingers at him, but he liked the lines. About how he'd like to be a wave because no matter how big the chunk of land, a wave would try to steal it away.

He'd hated being laughed at, and after that he'd kept his thoughts to himself.

Above the pounding of heavy seas, he heard noises. Men scampering like squirrels across the hatch cover. Their voices were hard to hear, but he sensed there was a manhunt on. They had decided he was aboard, but where in those huge dark holds they could not know.

They'd bide their time now, taking no chances against his gun, planning carefully to welcome him at the locks in Sault Ste. Marie. The whole police force plus the National Guard would turn out, and maybe a detachment or two from Canada, to make sure nobody goofed and let him escape.

Well, they didn't have him yet. Riggs Burkey had a sudden premonition that the ore boat would never make it to the Sault.

four

JIMMY MUNISING and the *Alyce* had weathered two days of stormy seas when he topped off the hold with one last giant lake trout and nosed the old tug back toward port. Whew! He was some tired. For several hours it had been man the bilge pump and haul in fish, as though the violent waves that washed the afterdeck had also dredged up lunkers from the depths. For the last hour there had been a lull; the winds had slowed to just over five knots, allowing the water to reflect the bright pink of scattered wind clouds.

He felt good. Eight—ten hours, depending on headwinds, he'd be back in port. Diane at the Brownstone Inn had offered to buy all the fish he could catch, probably never dreaming he'd head far out beyond the other boats and strike a bonanza like this. Make one last payment on the old fishing tug, and the *Alyce* would be free and clear.

He laid a caressing hand on the rail. Maybe the

Alyce was battered, weathered, wooden and old, without an ounce of chrome or one sporty curve to her utilitarian body. She'd weathered many a sea for many an owner, and that same slab-sided cabin that ruined her looks and caused tourists to run for their cameras kept her skipper dry and warm. He knew his mom would be proud.

The ancient single-cylinder Witte Diesel popped, hurtling a big blue donut of exhaust sideways across the waves, but the massive flywheel whirled on, sending an even, honest power to the screw regardless of whether or not the engine skipped a beat. Lars Jacobson, who had the garage over to Rock River, had helped him with the overhaul last winter in return for ten cords of dry maple for his sugarbush. New sleeve, rings and mainbearings too. Lars had stood patiently at his shoulder and helped him with details, but saw to it he learned how.

Suddenly impatient to head on home, Jimmy moved to the rear deck and reeled in his trolling downriggers. Land was nowhere to be seen, and the usual July throngs of sport boats did not venture this far out. The strange lull made it seem as though the winds were only holding back for a new assault.

He scanned the horizons to the south but saw nothing. Far to the northeast, he saw banks of clouds resembling a black continental mass of towering mountains. He shivered, wishing now that he had not quit the familiar waters over the Munising Trench and gone so far out on the lake.

However peaceful the water now seemed to him, he spotted trouble coming, an expanse of dark, indigo water between him and the clouds that spelled a vicious squall. He pushed the throttle up one more notch. The old engine knocked louder and did its best, but the dark clouds continued to come.

Off the starboard bow, he saw a flight of white-winged scoters, flying low, headed for some sheltered bay, perhaps toward Whitefish Point along the Michigan shore. They warned him that some even rougher weather was on its way, and he'd best hurry to shelter on Munising Bay.

The squall was on him suddenly; the cold wind sucked his breath away, and a savage chop enveloped the fish tug, but it was nothing the *Alyce* couldn't take in stride. Just the same, he picked up his trolling gear, lashed it down in the cabin, then latched the stern door against the renewing vigor of the storm. He was content now to remain inside.

For a moment, he fiddled with his short wave radio and picked up Caribou Light, some thirty miles south and east.

"Caribou Light, do you read me, Bert? This is your old pal, *Alyce* out of Munising. What we got coming up for weather out here on the pond? Over."

"Caribou. Yeah, I read you, Jimmy Boy. Nothing but bad news, Lad. Small craft warnings for the whole damn lake, and they predict it will get worse. Better light oot for safe harbor fast as that fat old tub can waddle. And Jimmy, don't pick up any hitchhikers.

"There's an ore boat, the *Charles H. Schaffer*, bound north of Caribou Island for Sault Ste. Marie. They figure that an escaped convict from the pen at Marquette has stowed away somewhere aboard. Better give me a fix on your position, Jimmy, and at least I'll let the Coast Guard know where to throw flowers over your bones. Come in, *Alyce*. Over."

Jimmy grabbed the wheel just in time to spin the *Alyce* out of a trough. The wind slammed at the walls of the cabin, rattling the windows in their frames, and the rear deck was suddenly awash with waves to the coaming.

"I say, Come in, *Alyce!*"

"Got my hands plumb full, Caribou. Get back to you in a few minutes, okay? Over."

"Caribou to *Alyce*. Better give it to me now, Jimmy. Things are getting busy. Over."

Jimmy reached back for the mike, but just then a giant powerhouse of a wave crashed over the cabin, and the next stood the *Alyce* on her nose. Unsecured, Jimmy's tool chest hurtled through the air, smashing the radio into silence; then, on the return, banged into the boy, bringing blood to his shins.

"*Bang, bang, bang,*" went the loyal old Witte engine above the screaming gale. The *Alyce* posed high on the crest of a wave, her propeller spinning uselessly in the air until she headed down into another trough.

The radio came on, heavy with static. "Caribou Light to the *Charles H. Schaffer*. I read you. Gale warnings escalating to storm warnings. Predict winds gusting to fifty knots and waves to twenty-six feet. Nearest port, Michipicoten Harbor. Beware Six Fathom Shoal off Caribou Island. Over."

Out of his port window, Jimmy suddenly spotted the bulk of a giant ore carrier looming close. In desperation he swung the wheel, and the fragile old fishing tug spun on her heel just in time to avoid being crushed like an eggshell.

"Hey, watch it!" Jimmy cried out as much to himself as to the command of the ship. He clung weakly to the wheel, pale as a ghost, peering out through windows aslop with wind-flung spray. First the forward deckhouse and pilothouse, topped with a radar screen like a hovering eagle, then the low-slung cargo areas, hatches awash with waves, then the after deckhouse and giant stacks belching out black smoke.

Jimmy scrambled for the mike. *"Alyce* to Caribou Light!"

"Caribou Light. Come in, *Alyce!"*

"Got to talk fast. My radio's beat to heck. Just saw your ore boat. Darn near ran me down. She's changing course, turning north toward Michipicoten. What if I get under her lee and ride along? Over."

"Caribou Light to *Alyce.* If you saw the *Schaffer,* Jimmy, you're a long ways from shore. What's the matter, you got sand for brains? As for tagging along, no way could your old tug keep up to stay under her lee. The Coast Guard has ordered all ships to find safe anchorage. I repeat, Jimmy. FIND SAFE AN-

CHORAGE! Forget Munising! Head east to get under the lee of Caribou Island, then head south along the west shore and make a run for my harbor here at the light. The missus says she has an extra bed until the storm blows over. Come in, *Alyce*."

A wave slammed the *Alyce* with brutal force and sent the radio skidding away from the boy. Slamming against a bulkhead, it sparked suddenly and shorted, erupting in blue flame as the wires arced and welded themselves together. Melted solder spattered on the floor; clouds of acrid smoke threw Jimmy into spasms of coughing. Shielding his eyes from the arc light he knew could blind him, he jerked the cable loose from the power source, and the flames flickered and died.

Left to itself, the wheel hummed. A heavy comber hurtled the *Alyce* through the air and dropped her creaking on her side. Trying to reach the wheel, Jimmy smashed hard against the cabin wall. As if by instinct, he fought back to grasp the wheel again and keep her from capsizing.

He peered ahead, knowing that he must keep track of the ore boat in the heavy seas. There she was, waves awash over her holds, pitching wildly as though she had lost her screw. Suddenly there was a violent tremor as earth and water seemed to quake. In front of the *Charles H. Schaffer* the huge trough of a mighty wave exposed the black of a reef and the giant ship dropped hard, struck the reef amidships and broke in two as though it were a child's toy. As the two ends listed helplessly, hatch covers flew open and a vast tonnage of taconite pellets spewed out into the gray churn of the sea. As he stared in horror and shock, Jimmy thought he saw the figure of a man hurtle doll-like from the avalanche of pellets into the icy waters of Lake Superior.

He felt nauseated and faint. In the tossing cabin, his eyes lost focus, and the howl of the tempest and the angry roar of the seas faded as he sagged to the cabin floor.

When he came to, the *Alyce* was chugging in circles, rocked by gentle swells, and the storm was a dull gray shroud hanging its gloomy curtains on the west. He pulled himself to his feet, felt a gash over his right eye, wiped his face with a fish towel, and hobbled out on the rear deck with his binoculars. Save for a few pieces of floating debris and a kaleidoscope of surface oil, there was no sign of the *Charles H. Schaffer.*

He made himself a cup of broth on the galley stove and felt better, then went chugging about from one island of flotsam to another, checking for possible survivors.

On an exposed reef, he found a lifeboat, upside down, a jagged hole battered in its hull. Nearby, a few thirty inch ring lifebuoys bobbed on the waves. He fished one out with his gaff. It had the name of the ship painted in large black letters, and he kept it as proof of what he had seen.

He had seen it, hadn't he? If only he could wake to find it had all been a dream! He was beginning to question his sanity. He longed to talk to the friendly old keeper on Caribou Light; with his radio gone, he'd better head there straight away and tell the lighthouse keeper of the tragedy.

five

JIMMY WAS ABOUT TO GIVE UP his search for survivors
and head for Caribou Light when he caught a flash
of white in the distance. It could have been a piece
of flotsam he had missed, or even a herring gull, but
when a human life might be at stake, he had to check
every floating object. As he came closer, he was glad
that he had not gone on. What he had seen turned
out to be a man's body, stretched out on a crude raft
of ring life buoys lashed together with nylon rope.
From his shoulders on down, the figure was covered
with a bleached canvas against the wind.

Jimmy could have sworn the man watched him as
the *Alyce* approached, but as the boy hove to, he saw
that the person lay unmoving on his stomach, cheek
on his forearm, eyes tightly closed.

"Hey," Jimmy called. "I've come to help you!"

The stranger did not move.

"You!" Jimmy hollered, wishing he were somewhere far away. "You alive?"

It looked as though he had a corpse on his hands. He put the *Alyce* in reverse and brought the afterdeck close so he could drag the body aboard.

A spasm of shivering shook the raft. The man was still alive! Turning away, Jimmy seized his gaff, but when he looked back, he found himself staring into the muzzle of a pistol.

"You!" The man hissed, forcing himself to his knees. His teeth were chattering uncontrollably, his voice rasping, and his eyes glazed with cold. "Toss me a rope or I'll use this thing! And no tricks!"

The raft lurched; the gun slipped from his grasp and almost tumbled into Lake Superior, but he pinned it against the raft, then fumbled it safely inside his shirt.

Jimmy had no doubt of the man's identity. The hitchhiker Caribou Light had warned him about. The boy calculated his chances. The man was almost out of it with hypothermia, halucinating with the cold, but dangerous. Woods-wise, Jimmy knew that a little moisture in the gun barrel might cause it, if fired, to blow up in the man's face, but Jimmy wasn't that ready to gamble. Another out was to drop to the deck behind the coaming and grab the remote control to the throttle, hoping the *Alyce* would surge forward, scooting the raft backward in a rush of prop wash. On the other hand, a single cylinder engine wasn't noted for its fast starts. And the point became moot anyway when he realized that the *Alyce* was in neutral.

He waited until the convict recovered from an

uncontrolled spasm of shaking, then tossed him a line. "Catch this, Mister," he said.

The prisoner snatched the yellow nylon out of the air, hauled himself in, and staggered aboard, dragging his raft up on the afterdeck. Slamming Jimmy against the wall of the cabin, he frisked him, then checked out the cabin. Smashing what was left of the radio with a kick, he rattled and banged through the cupboards for food, wolfing down a fistful of peanut butter cookies, then kicked off his wet prison dungarees, draping himself with blankets from the bunk.

"You, Kid!" he snarled. "Get some wood in that stove, and you got some dry clothes hidden away, trot 'em out!"

Sullenly, Jimmy moved to a closet, dragged out a pile of foulweather gear, and tossed the bundle on the bunk. "These clothes belonged to a previous owner," he said. "You might find something to fit." He went to the stove, added a couple of pieces of split cedar for quick action, then filled the rest of the stove with dry maple.

The convict sat on the bunk, pistol beside him, as he raked through the clothing. The gun didn't look so big and fearsome now. A finger shooter, a Saturday-night special, its chrome flaked away. He saw that the man's skin was waxen and death gray from the water.

"You need a doctor," Jimmy said. "Better let me head for Munising. Just getting you warm ain't the problem. Without the right treatment to get your circulation back, you might lose your hands and feet. Even die."

"No way!" the convict rasped. "I'll take my chances on the lake." The prospect of further captivity seemed to revive him. "Let's get out of here, Kid, and fast. When they figure out that ore boat ain't coming through the Sault Locks, the Coast Guard will fill the air with planes searching for her."

He pulled on some clothes and stood up to consult the big chart on the wall. "Where are we now?" he asked. "And no tricks."

Jimmy touched the map with the tip of his fore-finger. "Right here," he said. He could see no point in lying.

The man pointed to a small island northwest of Caribou Light. "What's this island called?"

"It ain't named."

"Who lives on it?"

"Nobody. Look for yourself at the chart and the soundings. Three fathoms and less. Surrounded by shoals marked 'Hazardous to Navigation'."

"Then head for her full throttle, you hear?"

A violent fit of shivering racked the big man, and he started to sit down on the bunk, but instead he pulled himself back up and stepped out on the af-terdeck. Tying his shirt, stenciled with his prison number, to the life raft, he set it adrift, then hurled the life buoys from the *Alyce* after.

"There," he said, satisfied. "The Coast Guard will

find these by morning and figure out just what I want them to—that you, me, this old tub, we all went to the bottom of the lake."

Jimmy's heart sank.

"Like they say," the convict went on, with a ghost of a smile, "Lake Superior don't give up its dead, not in that cold, cold water. Can't think of anything I'd like better right now than to have 'em write Riggs Burkey off the books as dead and gone."

Jimmy turned the fishing tug north, throttling it back as much as he dared, hoping that search planes trying to locate the ore boat would fly low over them and report that the *Alyce* had survived the storm, but was headed, strangely, away from Munising instead of toward it.

"Hey," Burkey complained, "can't this old wreck go any faster?"

"Not unless you want to risk throwing the rod," Jimmy replied, but he moved the throttle up another notch. Carefully, he eased the wheel to the right. A few degrees more off course and he'd circle past Caribou Light, and there was an off chance the lightkeeper might pick him up in his binoculars. In that lonely job, the keeper didn't miss much, and it would go down with meticulous accuracy that at such and such an hour, the *Alyce* had passed by heading north.

The wake betrayed him. The convict was no dummy. He looked out over the afterdeck, spotted the long, graceful curve of the wake, and turned back to catch Jimmy from behind, smashing him along side the head with a massive fist, sending him sprawling. Then he took over the wheel himself, peering frequently at the chart and the compass as though trying to figure how to use them.

They were in green water now, away from the debris and oil slicks that had marked the ore boat's grave.

Maybe he'll miss, Jimmy thought, lying quiet. *Maybe the island will be hidden by surface mists, and he'll pass on by. Way he's headed, he'll move into traffic—ore boats taking the long way because of the storm, or fishing craft operating out of Wawa on the Canadian shore.*

Jimmy had seen the island they were headed for in the distance the year before; it hadn't looked like much. No beaches on which to land; no harbors for waiting out a storm. Only cliffs waiting to punish boats who challenged her. During the Second World War, the Canadian Air Force had used the island for bombing practice, but now no one went there. Shallow-draught boats had no business so far from shore, and big boats avoided the shoals.

Whether they could land or not depended on the surf, and whether they could pick their way safely through the murderous reefs. Chances were that the big combers would break up on the shoals and only the chop would hit the island; but if there were no sandy beach, even small waves could be disastrous to the *Alyce's* thin lapstrake hull. He worried more about the safety of his boat than his own; she was all he had in the world. If there were no proper snug harbor, the *Alyce* would be crushed like an eggshell on the rocks.

A chill went through him. Maybe that was what Riggs Burkey intended! To kill him! To sink the *Alyce* without a trace, while he swam ashore!

A light breeze swept the mists away, and suddenly the island was there before them, gleaming green in the sun, less than a mile away. The convict throttled down the engine and cruised slowly, peering intently through Jimmy's binoculars, leaving nothing to chance.

Black, jagged reefs surfaced like sporting whales; the cliffs looks impenetrable. Midway down the east shore of the island, however, the man spun the *Alyce* about, then let her idle as he studied the situation.

"Get up there in the bow," Burkey ordered, "and watch for reefs."

"But you don't know how to navigate," Jimmy protested. "You'll ground her for sure!"

Burkey only glowered in return and, easing back on the throttle, headed the old tug toward shore.

Hanging from the bow, Jimmy saw immediately what had attracted the convict. Between the shoals, a stream of organic, coffee-colored water moved out to sea, indicating that from somewhere along those cliffs, an island stream moved out into Lake Superior.

Peering down into the murk, Jimmy shouted directions. "Hard to port!" he called. "Right! Right! Shoals dead ahead! Easy now. Hit the reverse. Now ahead. Easy to starboard."

Twice the channel ended and they had to retrace their route, but suddenly the brown water darkened, and Jimmy could see bottom sand among small multi-colored cobbles. Before them, the red sandstone cliffs opened to expose a narrow channel, which led to an inner harbor completely hidden from the furies of Lake Superior. As the *Alyce* chugged into the mouth of the stream, she passed over a sandy bar and on into a lovely sanctuary of quiet water.

Jimmy could see that the interior of the island was a world of its own, a large basin scattered with inland lakes, patches of boreal forest, and low sphagnum moss bogs of leatherleaf and Labrador tea. Black ducks flew up from the harbor's edge, and a pair of loons yodeled a protest to this intrusion.

It was a lost world. As the convict shut off the diesel engine and beached the prow on a spit of sand, Jimmy marveled at how suddenly Lake Superior had vanished behind them. Only the faint crash of surf on rocks came through the surrounding mute of balsam fir thickets.

Perhaps, centuries before, the island had been surrounded by beaches, but the eternal washing action of the waves had worn away the sands, leaving only cliffs. Sand remaining on the island had been scoured and blown into long north and south esters by prevailing winds, shifting with each great storm until seeds had migrated from the mainland, blowing in on the wind, rafting in on driftwood, or flying in stowed in the cargo hold of a bird. These adventurous seeds had stabilized the sands until the elements could no longer do and undo their handiwork at will, and the slow process of decaying vegetation gradually capped the sands with moisture-storing tilth.

The stream, which wandered across the island through sphagnum plains and leatherleaf bogs, had been colonized by beaver, who had dammed the sluggish drainages between esters into hundreds of small blackwater ponds and a scattering of larger lakes, before the water finally tumbled over the last dam to form the harbor where Jimmy and Riggs now stood.

Once the convict had loosed the anchor winch and sent the heavy weight splashing into the calm, he broke the glass covering the fire tools with a blow of his fist, plucked the axe from its holder, and tossed it to Jimmy. "Go cut us a pile of firewood," he ordered. "And don't go running off, either. You try to get away on this island and I'll hunt you down like a rabbit. You hear?"

"Yes, sir," Jimmy replied. As he moved off through tangles of leatherleaf and Labrador tea toward higher ground, Burkey tossed the tin chest of emergency rations ashore and methodically ransacked it, eating what he pleased.

Not far from the harbor, the boy found a dry log and set in chopping. Right now, he realized, he had no chance to escape. Best cooperate with Burkey and bide his time. It felt good to be out of the man's sight; he made the seasoned pine ring, knowing that the sound of his industry would reassure the convict.

Between every stroke of the red fire axe, however, he took in the lie of the land.

If Riggs Burkey had not been there, Jimmy might have relished the experience. Back from shore, the lowland brush gave way to carpets of blueberry plants, enticing the big yellow-and-black bumblebees with remnant danglings of pink bells. Wild raspberries and thimbleberries too prospered, giving promise of summer plenty. He picked up an armload of wood, carried it back to the fire, then picked a salad of dandelion greens and a pocketful of Labrador tea leaves for tea. He sensed the convict's total unfamiliarity with wilderness living and reasoned that the more useful he appeared to be, the greater his chances.

For the skipper of a small craft on the Great Lakes, part of coping with violent storms lay in seeking safe harbor and toughing it out. In a cupboard aboard the *Alyce* were the utensils basic to survival. Pots, pans, dishes, matches, canned and dried goods, and handiest of all, an iron grill that could be laid over a campfire.

As the man sat and watched, Jimmy unloaded his gear, then made a campfire on the sand. Propping the grill over the fire on rocks, he took a large lake trout from the hold, filleted it expertly, and placed the boned strips on the grill to broil.

As though tired from battling the storm, the *Alyce*, like a duck resting with head under its wing, nodded gently at her moorings. A blue kingfisher came rattling along the shore, orange belt natty on the immaculate whiteness of his waistcoat. He perched on the cabin of the boat as though it had been there always.

In the black spruces and balsams along the harbor, northern waterthrushes sang their territorial song, and Tennessee warblers flitted about the branches, gathering insects for young in the understory. Calm and clear, a white-throated sparrow fluted reassurance to Jimmy that the storm was over and that soon everything would be bright.

That evening, after they had gorged themselves on trout, Burkey locked himself in the cabin of the *Alyce,* while Jimmy slept out on a sand spit at the mouth of the harbor where a breeze kept the insects away. He wondered how soon planes would come, searching for the remains of the *Charles H. Schaffer.*

He lay watching the glowing embers of the campfire and tried to imagine the excitement the disappearance of a giant ore boat would cause. Not since the loss of the *Edmond Fitzgerald* in a November gale had there been such a disaster. Newspapers around the world would be full of it. Coast Guard planes, helicopters, and patrol boats would painstakingly comb that stretch of Lake Superior, picking up every shred of flotsam to read for clues as to what had caused the ship to go down. Inevitably, they would find the life rings from the *Alyce* as well as the convict's shirt on the raft. Given the realities of trying to survive on Lake Superior, it would be assumed that both he and the convict were dead.

"Please, God, don't let them believe I'm gone,"

he said, thinking of Alyce Marie, Alyce Ruth, and Alyce Anne.

But there was nothing he could do now but sleep. Fatigue numbed his senses; his eyes grew leaden, and he slept.

six

ONCE DURING THE NIGHT Jimmy awoke to the sound of distant aircraft high over the island, and the cloud cover glowed with flares dropped far out over Lake Superior. It was dawn when the sound of the latch being thrown on the cabin door and the creaking of planks on the afterdeck warned Jimmy that Burkey was awake.

"You, Kid. Up and at 'em. Build a fire and cook some more of that fish."

He was sitting on a log behind Jimmy, sharpening a knife he'd found on the *Alyce,* when the scream of demon laughter and an outburst of bloodcurdling wails cut loose behind them. Burkey whirled toward the sound, revolver poised, hammer back, ready to fire.

"What the hell is that?" he hissed.

Jimmy turned his face away to hide a grin. "Loons," he said. "Nothing but a pair of loons having a fight with the neighbors over territory."

Burkey set the gun down on the log beside him in readiness and kept glancing back over his shoulder as though he was not convinced.

"Come and get it," Jimmy called when the food was ready. He was not the best of cooks, but his fish was passable and the man's stomach bottomless. He watched carefully. As he hoped, the man left the revolver on the log as he approached the fire to help himself.

He's stupid! Jimmy thought. *He's falling right into my trap!*

The boy waited until the convict had loaded his plate with steaming fish, then edged toward the gun. Burkey seemed totally unaware of his actions. Once he had his captor covered, he'd hold him at gunpoint until he had the *Alyce*'s engine running and was headed out the narrow channel to safety. Just as Burkey sat down on a rock near the fire, Jimmy burst into action. He dove for the gun, seized it, and rolled away as he cocked the hammer. When he came to his feet, he had the revolver pointed at his enemy.

"Get your hands up, Mister, or I'll blow your head off!"

Riggs Burkey merely glanced at him and went on eating.

"I said, 'Get your hands up!'" Jimmy repeated, strain growing in his voice.

"Go ahead and pull the trigger," the convict said. "The gun's empty. You don't think I'd leave a loaded gun around where you could pick it up, do you?"

Jimmy's indecisiveness showed in his eyes.

"You don't believe me, Kid? See that dune over there? Squeeze one off. See if I'm lying."

Slowly, Jimmy swung the barrel about, aimed at a bush on the dune, and pulled the trigger. *"Bam!"* The revolver leaped in his hand, smoke curled, a shower of sand flew from the dune, and the bush, cut clean through at the base, toppled and rolled down the incline.

He turned the barrel back to Burkey. "Now, Mister. Get your hands up!"

The man took a mouthful of fish.

"I'm counting to ten," Jimmy threatened. "One! Two! Three!..."

"You used up the last bullet," Burkey said.

"You're lying!"

The convict's jaw set angrily. "Hell, pull the trigger, Kid. One thing Riggs Burkey don't like being called is a liar!"

Jimmy flipped open the cylinder the way Honest Risku had showed him once outside the store. Outside of one spent cartridge, the gun was empty.

Slowly, the big man set his plate down on the ground. He rose from the rock and came toward the boy, reaching out his hand for the gun. Jimmy thought of hurling the weapon far out into the pond and running for the brush, but he stood still, mesmerized by those smoke-gray eyes.

Riggs Burkey took the revolver slowly, gently by the barrel, twisting it from Jimmy's fingers, then exploded into action. Catching Jimmy below the temple with the butt, he knocked him backwards into the harbor, then stalked quietly back to the rock, took up his plate, and helped himself to more fish.

The cold water sucking into his lungs brought Jimmy to. Coughing and sputtering, he crawled half-way out of the water, then fell on the sand, not really caring whether he lived or died.

seven

JIMMY AWOKE TO THE SOUND of hammering. It came from the *Alyce;* and raising himself painfully on one elbow, he saw that Burkey had chiseled the name *Alyce* off bow and stern and was getting ready to paint her anew.

"You," he said, glancing at Jimmy, "take this bucket of paint and start slopping it on. We're painting this old tub blue."

Wobbly as a newborn colt, his head throbbing fearfully, Jimmy pulled himself dripping from the water and boarded the *Alyce.* He picked up the brush and bucket of paint and began working carefully, with long, even strokes, on the thirsty wood. He'd had that paint on board for months waiting for a time when he wasn't busy. Well, now he had plenty of time.

When he finished at day's end, his head still pounded and he would have liked to collapse in the sand and rest, but he knew better now than to be idle. The ice was beginning to melt in the hold, and the cargo of fish would soon spoil. Taking a fillet knife from the cabin, he sharpened it carefully, then began working on the fish, filleting out the bones, but leaving the two slab sides joined together at the tail in the manner of Indians. As he finished each fish, he hung it across a pole in the sun to dry.

It was dark when he finished the last of the fish, drained the hold of ice water, and scrubbed it down. Burkey sat silent on his log as though waiting for his supper. Jimmy wondered if the man knew how to cook over a fire. His headache had disappeared, forgotten about in hard work. He cooked up two large whitefish and marveled at the way Burkey stuffed himself until not a scrap was left.

Often during the next few days Burkey made trips to the bluffs overlooking Lake Superior to check for patrols that might have strayed from the area where the *Charles H. Schaffer* had gone down. Apparently satisfied that the search was finally over, he relaxed a bit; and if he climbed the headlands at all, it was to check weather conditions on the lake.

Now he seemed to take a sudden interest in botany, tramping the island to bring back roots and plants of various species. Great wilted armloads of pitcher plants, cattails, lady slippers, Clintonia, beach pea, mullein, and dandelion. All were dumped into a brew and simmered by the fire as Burkey peered hopefully into the steam. It was only when he added fistsful of iron oxide ooze from the marshes that the results seemed to please him.

With a knife, he cut off a lock of his hair and soaked it in the hot liquid.

So that's it, Jimmy thought. *He's painted the* Alyce *so folks won't recognize her; now he's going to dye his hair. I hope it all falls out!*

When the brew had cooled, Burkey washed his hair in it, turning his black locks and beard to a rusty brown.

"There, by God," he said. "They won't know me now!" He made a dozen trips to the mirror in the *Alyce,* reminding Jimmy of his sisters before a school prom.

He grabbed Jimmy by the arm, squeezing with his massive grip until it hurt. "You tell me the truth, Kid. I look different now, eh? You don't know me now."

"Know you? Where'd you come from? Where's that big black-haired guy was here just a few minutes ago?"

With a shove, he pushed Jimmy off his feet into a pile of brush. "Don't get smart with me, Kid. You hear?"

But he seemed pleased. He stood regarding the boy where he had fallen, looking down at him with a bemused expression, toying with the pistol in its shoulder holster. "I should put you out of your misery here and now, Kid, but I won't. You're useful to me as long as you behave. I'm planning to be gone now and then in your boat, and I need someone to tend camp." He laughed deep in his throat, tossing his auburn mane. "You be good, Kid, and maybe I'll bring you something nice from the store."

He stroked his beard thoughtfully. "While I'm away, you take your axe and cut me lots of straight logs, 'bout a foot through and long as your boat. Cut 'em any place on the island, but not right around camp. You savvy? While I'm traveling, I'll take me a good look at some log cabins to see how they're made, and when I get back we'll build us one for wintertime. Maybe I'll even bring back a nice wood stove to keep us warm."

Riggs Burkey cut himself a long slender pole, climbed aboard the *Alyce* and pushed off.

"One more thing, Kid. I see signal fires or even smoke coming from this island, and I'll come back and kill you for sure." He patted the butt of the revolver against his chest. "You understand me, Kid? You behave, and we'll get along."

Jimmy bridled at being called "Kid," especially since he was doing all the work. He gave Burkey his best glare.

"Yes, sir," Jimmy said. "Yes, sir."

eight

THE *ALYCE* HAD SCARCE DISAPPEARED around the jutting sandstone cliff into Lake Superior when Jimmy rushed up the slope to look down upon her. Turning this way and that, she floated like a feather amid the massive shoals, sailing first one channel then another, easing slowly but surely toward deep water. Now and then as she skirted a reef, he held his breath, hoping she wouldn't shatter and sink. One mistake on Burkey's part, and the *Alyce* would be gone, and with her Jimmy's only link with his past.

The boy had to admit that for all his lack of experience Burkey handled her well enough. He held her steady in the sliding sea while he carefully inspected the course for hidden dangers, sounding with his long pole here, using it to fend off rocks there, memorizing his route, backtracking often when he thought there might be a safer way. Actually running the *Alyce* was pretty simple; Burkey's worst troubles might come later, getting her to go if the fuel **line** sucked air and the fuel pump lost its prime.

Three hundred years before, Jimmy thought, fur traders might have learned of this harbor from the Indians, putting in for safety in their canoes. Perhaps more than once in the centuries, hunted men might have used the island for their hideout. But he doubted that in all of history any but desperate men would have dared those vicious shoals.

The boy breathed a sigh of relief as the *Alyce* moved past the last of the reefs and turned north at full throttle into a moderate sea. For a long time he sat and watched her until she disappeared into the low fogs chasing each other across the water, then rose to his feet.

Immediately he was busy, making use of each precious moment of freedom. Before Burkey returned, there were logs to cut, but those could come later. He rushed down to camp, took the axe, loaded his pockets with fish and hard biscuits, and took off following the island's shore.

The island was smaller than he had imagined, but also more beautiful. Back from shore, the stunted, ice-shattered trees gave way to virgin stands of balsam fir, black spruce, white pine, mountain ash, and birch. Now and then a lone pine had dared tower over the rest of the trees, but all too often it had paid the price for independence and had its top snapped off by the wind. Here on the island, trees seemed to flourish best when they hugged each other. From a ridge, he could see the little lakes, separated from each other by beaver dams, shallow end to deep, trailing each other down the valleys between the eskers. On each lake, a family of loons held court, each keeping a noisy fiefdom of its own.

Most of the loons had half-grown young. On one small lake, a tiny island of vegetation floated like an anchored raft, and here a loon had built her bulky nest of sphagnum, wild iris, water lily stems, and pitcher plants. She lay silent, head outstretched, hoping to be ignored by the boy standing on the shore. Nearby, her male cruised half submerged, uttering his tremolo. Jimmy waved to them and went on his way.

The mosquitoes and black no-see-ums seemed to be worst along the lowlands; the boy kept to the heights where the only menace were deer flies, which tangled themselves in his hair.

At the far end of the island, Jimmy found what he had been searching for: a small crevasse leading down an otherwise sheer cliff to a tiny beach of cobbles. Here he could make a small raft, hide it away from Burkey, and, when the time was ripe, sail away for freedom. Prevailing winds would take him in the general direction of Caribou Light.

Even if Burkey pursued him, he would not be putting the keeper and his wife in danger, for they could join him barricaded in the light tower, locked behind the heavy, vandal-proof steel plate door until their radio messages to the mainland for help were answered.

Just dreaming about such an adventure brought a grin to Jimmy's face. It would give the nice old keeper and his wife a story to tell in their retirement.

The boy took the axe and began felling balsam firs, cutting each trunk into raft-sized logs he could handle. What he lacked in size and strength, he made up for in determination. The limbs, he carefully threw over the cliffs to be swept away by the waves; the stumps, he buried under moss and forest duff. He did not dare peel the logs for fear they would stand out like bleached bones on the forest floor.

For crosspieces, fore and aft, to hold the raft logs together, he took a short fir log, cut wedges of birch, sharpened them, and drove them into the log until it split into two halves, each with a flat side. From a grove of black spruce, he selected a mast and two booms, which he carried to his growing cache of materials and covered with brush. Outside of some rope, a few spikes, and a piece of canvas for a sail, his materials lay there complete.

As he worked, he thought about the folks back in Munising and wondered how they were taking his apparent death. He pictured each of his sisters, Alyce Marie, Alyce Jane, and Alyce Anne, considering whether or not they would shed tears over him. Somehow it was easier to picture them smiling, with warm thoughts of the adventures they'd shared growing up, than mourning over his passing.

His jaw was still swollen from the convict's blow, and his eyes were misting with a touch of homesickness, but he wasn't one to dwell on his troubles. As he worked, he found himself whistling through swollen lips. He was all right. Escape was an adventure to look forward to. He had survived a wild storm on the big lake, capture by an escaped convict, incarceration on an uninhabited island, but mentally and physically he was still in one piece. He was Alyce's kid, and he had been raised to think that counted for something.

Now and again, he glanced out to sea, half expecting to see the *Alyce* putting in toward the harbor, but there was only an emptiness of waves, disappearing into the mists along the horizon. As though resting from the violence of that unseasonable storm, Lake Superior was putting on a spectacular show of good weather.

He had work to do before Burkey returned. In a grove of tall, slender balsam firs, a few hundred yards uphill from camp, he began felling trees, limbing them as they lay, cutting them into lengths, then stripping the bark in long shreds, exposing the immaculate whiteness of the wood underneath. It would have been easier to peel them in the spring, but he managed. His hands and face were soon black with pitch, which squirted from pockets on the bark, but its redolent odor seemed to keep insects away and soothe his blisters.

With what remained of the day, he cut and peeled eight logs; the next day he cut fourteen. Each night after a meal of fish, greens, and tea, he crawled to the heart of a huge pile of sphagnum moss and slept away his exhaustion.

By now he was enjoying his freedom so much, he hoped Riggs Burkey would stay away, but on the fourth day as he stood on the headland and scanned the lake, he saw the *Alyce* riding at anchor, waiting just beyond the shoals for the waves to subside with evening. Soon, in near calm, the *Alyce* came picking her way in and rounded the cliff into safe harbor.

Laden with cargo, the fish tug rode low in the water. Jimmy realized that the load had most likely been stolen along the Canadian shore, burgled perhaps from summer camps whose owners lived elsewhere. A rifle, boxes of ammunition, blankets, splitting mauls, adzes, sledges, wedges, spikes, roofing materials, hand saws, even a brand-new canoe. And food. Tons of it. Whole sides of bacon and cases of canned goods. The groceries, at least, were covered by a receipt from a Wawa market. No matter. No doubt Burkey had stolen the money and shopped at his leisure. To the folks in the store, he must have seemed like any other backwoodsman stocking up for months in the bush.

While the man rested from his journey, Jimmy sweated away at unloading the ill-gotten cargo and storing it in a fissure in the sandstone bluff above camp.

"Don't go looking so hard at that canoe, Kid," the convict snapped. "It ain't your ticket to anywhere. I got uses for it, and whenever I leave on that tug, the canoe goes with me."

Jimmy could well imagine how useful a canoe could be to a burglar. He could anchor the *Alyce* off shore, wait for darkness, slip in to commit whatever robbery he had planned, and make his getaway. According to authorities, Riggs Burkey now would be dead, and besides, who would be expecting a burglar to make his getaway by water?

The boy started to unload ammunition, but the big man stopped him. "That stays aboard," he commanded. "You can be damned sure I'll keep guns and ammo locked in the hold to keep you out of mischief. That stuff is my travel insurance. Nobody's going to take that old tug from me without a helluva fight!"

nine

THE NEXT MORNING, Burkey ordered Jimmy to accompany him back into the forest. With a critical eye, he inspected each of the cabin logs the boy had cut. He seemed pleased that a boy Jimmy's size had been able to produce so many logs with only a hand axe.

"Got callouses to prove it," Jimmy said, holding up hands, which had already passed beyond the blister stage. He thought to himself that the convict would be even more impressed if he knew that Jimmy's output, all cut and ready, included a pile of raft materials hidden under brush at the far end of the island.

Along one of the bogs, thickets of cattail grew, the round shoots straight and tall. Burkey cut two big armloads, lopped off the seed heads, and loaded Jimmy down, packing the rest himself. Chopping the stems into short, even lengths, he sent Jimmy back into the woods to cut more cabin logs, while he sat in the shade, back to a rock, patiently notching, trimming, and shaping the stems into miniature logs with which to build a cabin model.

Perhaps Burkey had looked at several cabins along the north shore of Lake Superior, but there were things he had failed to notice. The first model took him all morning to construct and was so ill-conceived it fell into ruin just as Jimmy happened back into camp to cook lunch. Burkey glared as though it were Jimmy's fault.

Jimmy, who had helped Lars Jacobson build a log cabin and sauna along the Rock River and knew perfectly well how to build with logs, wasn't about to make helpful suggestions. On the other hand, Riggs Burkey, a product of Detroit streets, had no inkling of the stores of useful information a country boy puts by just growing up and didn't consider seeking information.

There was in the man, however, the persistent nature of the craftsman. By evening, Jimmy was surprised that Burkey had not only constructed a good, sound model, but had thought up a few innovations unheard of among the Finns and Swedes who had settled Lake Superior's shores.

Jimmy had trouble even budging the heavy green logs, so Riggs Burkey made himself a rope harness, attached a trace to each log, and skidded it down the hill to the cabin site. When all the logs for the walls had finally been decked to dry, he dragged in slabs of sandstone strata from the cliffs, breaking them with hammer and chisel, or grinding them with rocks and water, until they fit so tightly into a foundation for the cabin that not even a mouse could have squeezed through. Apparently breaking rocks was something the convict had done before.

It seemed to Jimmy that the convict worked so slowly and painstakingly that it would be winter before the shelter was built. He, himself, had no intention of staying on the island long enough to need a cabin, but he reminded himself again and again that his best chance for survival lay in making himself useful to Riggs Burkey, and so he pitched in and helped whenever he could.

Indeed it was hard to do nothing. Growing up, he had been active with school during the day and jobs after, with weekends spent fishing the big lake. He longed to be back on the *Alyce* traveling somewhere, anywhere, and even the thought of rafting away from the island filled him with excitement. Spirits buoyed by coming adventure, he kept busy every waking hour.

By now the wild raspberries had ripened and the bushes were loaded with small, sweet fruit. Jimmy could not resist taking off time to pick, and Burkey often went with him, squatting in the midst of a patch of bushes, raking in fruit like some huge, cranky cinnamon bear. He did not add much, however, to the camp larder, for he ate most of what he picked.

What they could not eat, Jimmy spread out in

thin layers on blankets to dry in the sun. During lean times, they could eat the dry berries as fruit, or grind it with meat to make that staple of northern trappers, pemmican.

Dawn to dusk, when not picking berries, they worked on the cabin. Burkey was a harsh taskmaster. Jimmy soon learned that when the convict wanted a tight fit, he meant just that. He allowed the boy to notch the logs while he held them, but each notch had to be uniform and fit perfectly with another.

The big man himself made a specialty of using the foot adze, flattening opposite sides of the logs so that they fit together snugly, leaving a minimum of cracks. One of Burkey's innovations was to lay two twisted sphagnum moss ropes parallel with each other along the flat upper face of the top log, so that the weight of the next log crushed down upon it and made an effective seal with an air pocket up the middle.

Often Burkey rejected a log as unsuitable, and then Jimmy was sent back into the woods to find another. The new log had better be straight or the convict would be in a foul mood the rest of the day.

By mid-August, the walls were up, and Burkey took Jimmy out in the woods and set him cutting good straight rafters of spruce without galls or blemishes. He took off again in the *Alyce,* with the warning that the poles would all have to be cut, peeled, and decked by the time he returned or there would be hell to pay.

The *Alyce* was barely beyond the reefs when Jimmy

borrowed a long nylon rope and handful of spikes from Burkey's cache and raced through the woods toward the cove at the north end of the island.

To his relief, the logs remained where he had hidden them. One by one, the boy rolled them out of the forest to the cliff above the cove and let them tumble to the cobble beach below. The mast, spars, and crossties followed after. Then, once the materials were dropped, he fastened the rope to a sturdy birch and rappelled down the cliff.

Carefully, he peeled the bark from the logs to hasten their drying and add to their buoyancy. In each of the two center logs, he cut a matching notch to accomodate the butt of the mast. Fitting the tall, slender spire into place, he spiked it into the first log, then pried the other center log into position. An hour later the raft was almost done, and the crosspieces spiked into place. The mast gleamed tall and straight like that of some old pirate ship. Except for a pulley for the top of the mast and some sail material to lash to the spars, he was set for his escape.

It would not be easy, he knew. Surf welled between two black, moss-encrusted boulders, invading the tiny cove, and seemed eager to reach the new craft and destroy it even before it sailed. Storms like those that formed the cove might once again sweep across Lake Superior without warning, and the cove itself would be gone.

But that was a chance he would have to take. Using a pole as a lever, he pried the raft up as far as he could under the protective overhang so that it could not be seen from above, then covered it bow to stern with driftwood. Once he had camouflaged the mast with fir boughs, he hauled himself up the face of the cliff on the rope and returned it to Burkey's cache.

ten

IN THE DAYS THAT FOLLOWED, Jimmy avoided the north cove, but worked hard, felling, limbing, and peeling the tall, slender poles he cut for rafters. As he finished each piece, he dragged it to the cabin and stacked it against the others to dry in a pile resembling a wigwam.

After six days the convict returned to the area, but it was another two days before the heavy seas calmed enough to let the *Alyce* in past the shoals. Jimmy could see the Alyce riding at anchor, pitching and tossing wildly in the storm; having ridden out such waves himself, he grinned, knowing just how seasick the convict must be.

When Burkey returned, he was pale as a ghost and mean. He inspected Jimmy's work carefully, as though trying to discern whether Jimmy had worked at cutting rafters the whole time or spent some hours working on an escape project.

He found fault with several of the rafters, where

burls Jimmy had peeled away with the axe showed weak spots. Such a rafter might buckle under a heavy load of winter snow. With a growl, he ordered the boy back into the woods, and while Jimmy cut and peeled replacements, the convict worked at unloading plunder from the *Alyce*'s hold.

He had gone south this time, Jimmy decided, probably figuring that the Canadians might be watchful. From stencils on the side of a packing box, Jimmy realized that the groceries, at least, had come from Munising, maybe from Horus Matson's store. Most likely he had left the *Alyce* riding at anchor in the darkness well up the shore while he had made a foray on the town by canoe.

Once, as Jimmy passed dragging a pole, Burkey staggered ashore carrying an immense carved oak door, which bore a weathered brass plate inscribed "THE RECTORY."

"Took it right off the preacher's house on Sunday morning," the convict boasted. "I could hear the damn fool preaching hellfire and damnation in the church right next door."

Next came a bundle of several clotheslines full of clothes, clothespins and all. Some were loaded with ladies' apparel, indicating that Burkey had made those heists in the darkness, hoping for some clothes he could wear.

Jimmy's eyes gleamed as he saw a case spilling over with bright blue nylon tarpaulins edged with brass grommets. All he needed was one of those and he'd have a great sail for his raft!

The last item on board was heavy enough that even in its stripped-down condition, it gave the powerful Burkey trouble as he tried to unload it. It was a large Majestic wood stove, beautifully decorated in gleaming chrome. In a pile on the shore were the lids, warming ovens, and a tank for heating water. Beside these were the heavy cast iron grates. Burkey had taken some time with that project, stripping the stove to make it manageable.

The convict had stolen a dolly along with the stove. It was a heavy, two-wheeled unit, almost useless in sand. On the back was stenciled "Property of Huron Mountain Club." Apparently the man was working miles of shoreline in each raid. The club was an exclusive private resort some sixty miles up the coast from Marquette. He pictured Burkey poling the *Alyce* silently into the mouth of the river at the club, backing up to an unguarded dock, stealing the stove from the camp while the owner was away, and trundling it right down a boardwalk to the dock and onto the deck of the *Alyce* while the resort slept.

"You, Kid! Help me get this beast ashore," Burkey snapped.

They laid a ramp of heavy planking from the rear deck of the *Alyce* to the beach on which to wheel the stove. The planks strained under the hard rubber dolly wheels, and once they almost upset the load into the water, but Burkey managed to steady the stove just in time. By laying planks along the beach, they were able to move the stove to more solid ground under a big pine tree.

The *Alyce* was heavily laden. Sweat ran down Jimmy's cheeks as he worked, and now and then he dove into the pond with his clothes on to cool himself. There were boards for the cabin roof, gables, and floor, bundles of wooden shakes, rolls of tar paper, sheets of aluminum flashing for around the stove pipe hole and the gutters. Windows, complete with frames and hinges, pots and pans, sacks of ready-to-mix concrete. Everything the cabin needed, including cupboards, tables and chairs. Even a bed and mattress for Burkey and a cot for Jimmy. Jimmy could guess at the furor there would be on shore when all this turned up missing.

It was almost dark when they finished stacking the last of the cargo and covered it against the weather with the tarps. There was one left in the case, and Jimmy eyed it thoughtfully, glancing over at Burkey to see if he were watching. The man stood looking at him, and Jimmy had the odd feeling that the convict could read his escape plans written plain as day across his face. The boy moved quickly down the hillside to the camp and occupied himself with cooking supper.

During the night, a warm rain fell, and in the morning ghosts of mist drifted across the inland lakes. Burkey hardly touched his food, but seemed impatient to be off again. He clambered aboard the *Alyce*, checking the canoe lashings, changing oil in the engine, filling the grease cups, things he had never trusted Jimmy to do.

As the convict shoved off, Jimmy busied himself

splitting kindling, pretending not to notice as the *Alyce* slid around the base of the cliff and was gone.

Excitement welled within Jimmy. The time for his escape had come to him sooner than he expected. Overjoyed to be out from under the brooding gaze of his captor, he rushed to the headland. There was the *Alyce,* already through the reefs and in open water. Lake Superior was running a beautiful green sea.

"Yippee!" Jimmy shouted, starting the loons to chorusing up and down the island.

The seas out there were rougher than he would have chosen for rafting, but the wind looked right. He could sail before the wind to Caribou Light and freedom. Freedom! What a day to be free!

Hugging himself in excitement, he rushed back down to the camp and raided the supplies. So sure was he that he would never see the place again, he paused to kick Riggs Burkey's bedroll full of wet sand.

Grabbing up some food for his journey, he stuffed the pockets of his jacket, then took the last tarp from where Burkey had hidden it in one of the warming ovens of the stove. Once he had picked up a supply of nylon rope from the cache, he hurried off into the forest without a backward glance at the camp.

He was out of breath when he reached the north end of the island, but he could rest later. He found a heavy pry pole, threw it over the cliff, then followed on the nylon rope, pulling it down the cliff after him in a final act of commitment.

Threading rope through the grommets on the tarp,

he lashed one spar to the bottom and the other to the top. Then he tied a rope to the top of the upper spar, lashing it carefully so it would not slip.

In the top of the mast, in the likelihood he would never find a pulley, he had cut a V large enough to hold the rope. In his eagerness, it took several throws to get the rope into the V, but when he finally succeeded, he pulled one end of the rope, drawing the spar and sail up the mast into position, and tied it fast to the raft.

The blue nylon sail spanked sharply in the wind as though impatient to be off. Carefully, he anchored the bottom spar to the mast with a loop. "It's going to work!" he said with a chuckle. "Caribou Light, here we come!"

He had a funny feeling someone was watching from above, but when he looked up along the cliffs, he saw nothing unusual. From somewhere back in the forest, a raven croaked, and the shore wind sighed in the branches of the white pines overhead. A flock of cedar waxwings, sleek and immaculate in new plumage, landed in the crown of a massive mountain ash and sampled a few orange berries before flying off again over Lake Superior toward some distant destination.

The sail guttered and slapped, and the mast creaked under the strain. Jimmy slid his pry pole under the heavy raft and pried it away from the cliff. Waves lapped against the logs; one more heave and the raft would be launched! In four hours he could make Caribou Light!

A small pebble fell from the cliff above and bounced off the deck of the raft into the lake.

Startled, Jimmy glanced upwards but could see nothing. He was about to give the raft one final heave, when a larger rock came crashing down, catching the bellying sail and ripping a jagged hole. Peering down the cliff was Burkey, his face dark with rage.

Jimmy had only a split second to leap for safety as the convict put his shoulder to a huge boulder and toppled it downward over the cliff, dislodging an avalanche of smaller rocks as it fell. There was a splintering crash as the raft disintegrated and was buried under a ton of rubble.

Too stunned to weep, Jimmy leaned backward against the cliff. He had been outwitted. Burkey had suspected that he was up to something and had taken the *Alyce* out for a short spin, intending all the time to double back and check his activities.

Burkey said nothing, but signaled for the rope. Obediently, the boy threw it up to him, then caught the end as it swayed past him in the wind, and let the convict swing him up over the rocks.

eleven

PIECE BY PIECE, the roof went up. First Burkey set an upright atop the logs at each end of the cabin, then topped these two uprights with a heavy ridgepole. Carefully, he fitted the butts of the rafters into the top of the side logs, allowing for eaves, and laid the small ends to peak over the ridgepole, closing in the gables with rough pine boards. Over the rafters, he nailed a roof of the same material as the gables, then covered it with a double layer of roofing paper, followed by a covering of wooden shakes.

The man worked slowly and deliberately, making everything tight. When he finished setting the lovely old rectory door in the front wall of the cabin, it looked as though it had been custom made for the hewn frame. The windows fitted so snugly into the walls there was scarcely any room to wedge in moss.

Only when the cabin shell was almost complete, did Burkey turn to installing a floor. To the underside of the heavy, hand-hewn spruce floor joists, he nailed sub-flooring, which he covered to the top of the joists with dry sphagnum moss for warmth. Over this layer of moss went several layers of building paper capped with sub-flooring laid diagonally, two more layers of building paper, regular flooring laid parallel, finished off with odds and ends of linoleum he'd collected, no two remnants the same.

"There," Burkey said, contemplating his work. "I suppose a good carpenter would a done it different, but anyway that'll be hell for snug."

Once the floor was in, the next concern was the big stove. Because the cabin was on a knoll considerably above the shoreline of the lake, moving the big Monarch up the hillside was no easy matter. Under all that weight, the dolly wheels sank immediately in the soft dirt. Only by building a track of planking, tearing up each section after the stove had passed over and laying it down in the area immediately in front, were they able to worry the stove up the hill.

Soon the first wisp of smoke rose above the roof from the stove pipe; and that evening, for the first time since their arrival at the island, they ate a stove-cooked meal. The insects that had plagued them since their arrival thronged the outside of the window panes but were unable to get in.

The fact that they now had a roof over their heads did nothing to lessen Jimmy's determination to escape. Any scheme, no matter how remote its chance of success, was better than no scheme at all.

During the late summer evenings, he set about

carving a model sailing ship, complete with sails and weighted keel. Burkey watched the project from afar but could find no fault with it. Jimmy gave the ship its first launching in the harbor below camp and was thrilled to see how gracefully the sails filled as the ship ran with the breeze. The keel kept it upright in the wildest of surfs.

He stole a rifle bullet Burkey dropped in the sand and cut a square of white birch bark parchment from the forest. Using the lead tip of the bullet to write, he inscribed on the bark:

SOS. Held prisoner by convict on unnamed island N.W. Caribou Light. Has commandeered my fish tug, *Alyce* of Munising. Armed and dangerous. Camped at S.E. corner of island, where inland stream runs out through cliff face, into Lake Superior. Dangerous shoals.

Jimmy Munising

Sealing the parchment in a jar, he lashed it to the deck of his little ship for added buoyancy; then, when the convict was working on the interior of the cabin, he half waded, half swam out through the channel, pushing the tiny boat before him, until the wind caught its sails, and it went bobbing off on its own into Lake Superior.

A heavy sea threw a chop into his face, and the clear green waters were like ice compared to those of the island's inland waterways. A steady wind filled the sails, and the little ship braved the surf, sailing steadily southward, all but lost in the troughs between the waves. The chances were one in a million that the square rigger would survive to beach on an inhabited shore where some beachcomber would find the note and turn it over to the authorities. But he had to try.

During the next few days, he stole every opportunity to mount the headland and check the prevailing winds on the big lake. In that he was lucky, for a steady breeze blew from Canada; by his calculations, that would land his ship somewhere between Munising and Marquette, where there were still summer people around to find it.

If the convict noticed that the ship was gone, he did not mention it. He worked steadily, moving furniture and dishes into the cabin from the cache, until the place looked lived in.

When the cabin was complete, he seemed to relax a little, even taking time to explore the inner island, where only the crash and boom of far-off surf indicated that Lake Superior existed.

Burkey said little. If he wanted the boy to come with him in the canoe, he simply picked up one end and stood waiting patiently until Jimmy picked up the other. They paddled silently, with Burkey in the stern, setting the pace, steering them through a wild world. The loons came to accept their quiet presence; the birds moved only a little way from their path before they went again about their business, trailing their broods.

Once as they explored a beaver pond neither of

them had seen before and drifted quietly watching the forest mirrored upside down on the utter calm before them, a mother loon swam by with two young still trying to steal a ride on her back. Partly grown, the young were heavy cargo and kept submerging the ship. For the first time, Jimmy heard Burkey laugh. It may be that such a sign of weakness embarrassed the convict, for he did not say a word the rest of the day.

The canoe trips, portaging from one lake to another, were all the fun the convict allowed himself. If he spoke occasionally, it was to ask Jimmy the name of a bird they saw; and, once told, he never asked again. Often he sat quietly in the stern, paddle across his knees, watching the wildlife about him. To Jimmy, the island was captivity; but to the convict, used to years in prison, it must have seemed like total freedom.

The trips in the canoe did not fool Jimmy. He realized that Burkey did not take him along for company or to help with the portages. The big man could handle the canoe like a toy all by himself. He could not trust Jimmy alone around the *Alyce;* he knew Jimmy would use any chance he got to try to escape.

By now the blueberries had ripened and the timber edges were blue with them. Jimmy picked them by the gallon, drying them in the sun as he had the raspberries in their season. They ate them fresh every meal of the day, and Jimmy became an expert at turning them into pies. Even dried, they turned his morning muffins into an experience.

Once the first frost turned the blueberry leaves scarlet, Burkey left the island again. The batteries on the *Alyce* showed corrosion on the terminals, and in the colder weather of autumn, they hardly turned over the engine. It was sometimes noon before the old Witte Diesel would start.

"You want that rig to run for you," Jimmy ventured, "you better go to the mainland for new batteries. And while you're there, put new antifreeze in the radiator. Wouldn't surprise me out here on the island what with chill factor, she might hit fifty below."

The antifreeze was still good, he knew, but he needed Burkey off the island for a while. For a long time after the *Alyce* disappeared into the autumn haze, Jimmy watched. He had no intention of having Burkey surprise him again.

Lake Superior looked gray and dangerous out there. It was not the time of year to try to cross her in a small boat, but that was exactly what Jimmy intended to try. Right at the moment, of course, he didn't have the boat, but that wasn't the worry. The other day when he'd been out gathering firewood for winter, he'd rapped on a big old white pine with his axe and found it hollow as a pumpkin.

Chances were that Burkey would try to buy the heavy-duty marine batteries for the *Alyce* in Wawa, instead of going to the Sault. That would be safest; but most likely the man who ran the marina along the river where the convict would dock would have to order them, and that would take a few days. In about six days of hard work, Jimmy thought, he could shape a section of the trunk of the old white pine into a pretty fair sailboat and be gone.

Burkey had taken most of the tools with him in the *Alyce,* but he had forgotten a brace, a ship's auger, a bow saw, and a foot adze, all a boatmaker really needed. Certainly Indian craftsmen had had a lot less.

One of his precious days Jimmy spent felling the giant pine. He carefully dropped the tree upslope to lessen the impact when it fell. Even so it dropped with an earth-shaking roar, covering the land about with a pall of red dust from its rotten core.

Great slabs of bark fell away, revealing the tubes and tunnels of a host of insects who, invited in by old age, had done the old pine in. Jimmy climbed the fallen trunk and walked slowly down its length. A great fat woodborer grub, lying exposed and helpless on its back, peered up at him, waving stubby legs in an effort to right itself.

Thirty feet from the butt of the log, he found what he wanted. A huge limb, three feet thick, jutted from the main trunk and, though broken off four feet from the main trunk, appeared to be intact.

"One step at a time," the boy told himself to calm his beating heart. "Got to cut off every scrap of wood I can't use, get rid of every ounce of weight I don't need so I can move this thing down the hill to water."

Methodically, he marked long sloping cuts for bow and stern, visualizing the branch as a keel. He would have liked to add more length and slope, but that meant a longer saw cut, a longer opening, and there was only so much planking left over from making the cabin to use for boarding in the ends. And so he compromised for the practical, took the bow saw, and began the slow process of sawing away the excess wood.

Daylight to dark he worked, scarcely taking time out to eat. One precious day gone shaping the hull, another cleaning the rotten wood out of the center. He worked the inside of the hull with the adze, then rolled the log a turn or two down hill to dump out the shavings. Then back to work with the adze, hewing the hull just as thin as he dared. The sound of the adze made a muffled drumbeat through the forest.

Once the hull was off the steep slope, the keel made it impossible to roll by hand, so he resorted to pry poles, to lever the log down to the water's edge. By now he knew every foot of the vast network of beaver runs and waterways and, with only one brief portage, was able to float the log down to Burkey's harbor.

Time was running out, and he worked feverishly. Propping the hull on its back on the beach, he planked up bow and stern, cutting off the excess with the bow saw. He spiked a piece of planking across the opening of the keel so he could fill the hollow with rocks for ballast. Then, after melting a bucket of spruce resin on a fire, he applied the the sticky stuff liberally to the seams, filling the larger cracks with a dough of resin and sphagnum moss. When, at last, he rolled the boat over into the water to soak, he was thrilled to see that it floated like a cork on the calm surface of the little harbor.

There was no time, however, to stand around admiring his handiwork. Burkey might be back any hour. He cut a mast and two spars, then fitted a sail. A little primitive perhaps, but sleek, too. Here was a ship that could run! Excited, he ran to the cabin for blankets, extra rope, and food, throwing in a couple of extra tarps, one for shelter, the other for a sail in case he lost the original.

Shoving off, he poled the craft around the bend into the surf of Lake Superior.

twelve

SPUME LEAPED AT HIM from the rocks, and the wind sucked his breath away. Beyond the snug cove, Lake Superior seemed to be running wild with a fall norther. Desperately, he seized the rudder pole and tried to push back into the harbor, but a gust, caroming off the cliffs, combined with a retreating wave to smash the boat into a reef. The hull boomed like a drum but miraculously held. Spinning into a vortex, the boat lurched over on its side as the keel ground against rocks, then rose high again with a swell. For the first time in his life, Jimmy was frightened of the raging sea.

With one more thrust of the pole, he managed to avoid the reef. No choice now but to head out into the churn of waves. Away from the chop along the shore, things might be better. The cold wind numbed his wet hands, and the rough bark on the pole tore a patch of skin from his knuckles, but he was too chilled to bleed.

He glanced down at his feet, half expecting to see water surging into the boat, but his caulking job was holding well. The unknown bothered him. He longed for the familiar deck of the *Alyce* beneath his feet. The Alyce would have taken this sea in stride; but this hastily constructed craft pitched and bucked with each whitecap, so that he had to cling to the mast for balance.

The last reef slid by, inches away, and suddenly the pole lost contact with the bottom. Crawling back to the stern on hands and knees, he inserted the pole through a rope loop, extending it into the water behind the craft as a rudder. He marveled that even without hoisting sail, the ship came about and steadied, scudding along like a leaf before the wind.

Out beyond the reefs, he dared half a sail, then pulled a tarp over his body and huddled down in the hull out of the wind, holding only the rudder as the boat planed across the tops of the waves, headed toward Caribou Light and safety.

On the island he hadn't let himself think about school, but now he began to be excited. He pictured himself strolling in to the principal's office, with a casual, "Sorry I'm late." Late? By now he must be a couple of months late. But they'd have to forgive a hero.

He grinned to himself as he pictured Burkey's face as he returned to the island and found him missing. There would be no safe haven for the man, once Jimmy made it to Caribou Light, and the keeper took to his radio to let the world know that Riggs Burkey was still alive.

Jimmy had just changed arms over the rudder pole when he glanced back for one last look at the island. The mists hid the distant cliffs, but off to the north, he caught a flash of bright light. It was the *Alyce,* and the flash had to come from Burkey's binoculars catching sunlight. He realized that Burkey must be trying to discern what strange manner of craft this was defying the icy winds so far from shore.

Jimmy thought of dropping his sail to make a lower profile, but suddenly he saw the *Alyce* grow small as she turned from broadside to face him, and the boy knew his race was on. Raising full sail, he pulled his knit cap down low as his new ship fairly skimmed across the waves.

"He won't get me!" the boy vowed. He shifted his rudder pole as the wind changed and was forced to lean out over the waves to keep the sail out of the water. Everything he had ever learned about sailing was important now. One mistake and the icy waters would have him, and Burkey's secret would be safe.

Slowly but surely, the *Alyce* was gaining on him. One of the grommets in his sail ripped out, letting slip some of the wind. Another grommet was showing strain. There was nothing he could do but hope that the rest held. Already in the distance he could see the lighthouse tower like a great shining white rocket being readied for a shot at the moon.

First Burkey was a quarter of a mile away, then three hundred yards. Jimmy expected to see the lightkeeper moving to the pier to welcome him. There was no way now he could change tack and stay ahead of the *Alyce.* Best run his boat straight into the rocks, leap for it, and head straight for the tower to lock himself behind the iron doors.

He heard the old Witte on the *Alyce* backfire and looked back to see her in trouble. Heavy smoke billowed from her exhaust, and as she lost momentum she turned broadside to the wind. His heart leaped. The engine had blown its injector and would sit right there until Burkey could manage to put in a new one.

Jimmy changed tack, sailing quite comfortably now, skirting the tiny island to hit the harbor and slide in behind the concrete breakwater.

There was not much on the island in the way of buildings. Just the great tower with its bank of reflectors made in France, built to guide ore boats past the shoals toward the Sault. A small white house with red roof for the keeper and his wife. A few matching buildings spotlessly kept, which housed the generators for the island's electricity. A harbor for the tender, which came intermittently from its base in Ontario to service the light.

As he slid behind the island, his last glance at the *Alyce* showed that Burkey had somehow replaced the injector, bled the lines of air bubbles, and was once more underway. Jimmy plowed into the dock, leaping to grab the iron railing, abandoning his craft to the waves. Scampering across the brown lawn toward the keeper's house, he charged up the front steps and hammered on the door, listening all the time for steps inside. The house was silent. He tried the latch.

It was locked! The keeper and his wife were gone, the light closed for the winter season.

Unbelieving, he rushed to the tower, hoping to slip inside and bolt the heavy iron doors behind him. But they were already locked tight against vandals. Orders of the Crown.

He started to run again for the dock, to leap for his ship, fully ready to brave the storm and make a run for the Sault. But as he gained the concrete harbor, he saw the *Alyce* catch his sailboat amidships and splinter her into driftwood. Burkey leaned patiently back against the aft rail and waited for him to surrender.

thirteen

IT WAS DARK WHEN THEY finished unloading the *Alyce* in the harbor. Among the treasures Jimmy saw was a collection of antique Coleman lamps, all of them needing repair. The boy grumbled over their condition, but in another box he found an assortment of new generators, mantles, wrenches, pumps, leathers, and other parts, enough to restore the grand old lamps to mint condition. And Burkey had even thought to bring along a bright new drum of white gasoline.

Jimmy would have liked some reading material, but all he found was a worn and dog-eared copy of Richard Pough's *Audubon Guide to North American Birds*. He set it carefully aside for evening, but that night when he had lit the cabin with one of the lamps, and the supper dishes were put away, he looked for the book and found that Burkey had already usurped it and sat on his bed looking at the illustrations. The big man shook his head as though in disbelief that there were so many different varieties. Later, when he went to bed, he put the book under his pillow as though hoping to absorb all the information in the book by some sort of osmosis.

Not long afterwards, the inland lakes glassed over with ice, and the leaves fell from the deciduous trees.

"Be the last trip out," Burkey said, standing on the headland looking out over the gunmetal gray of Lake Superior. Twice already they had awakened to a light blanket of snow on the ground. It had been gone by noon, but it had reminded them that they had better be ready for winter.

"Long time before spring," the convict went on. He was not generally so loquacious.

Jimmy welcomed the prospect of being alone and did not comment. But he was ever watchful as Burkey prepared for his trip. Waiting for the man to make a mistake, for the break to happen and the chance for freedom to arrange itself.

The convict started the *Alyce* and let her warm up at a fast idle, held in place by a rind of ice on the harbor. Jimmy was cutting up a windfall for winter firewood a short distance from the camp when the man came out on the afterdeck of the tug, looked carefully for the boy and, observing that Jimmy was busy some distance away, moved uphill to the cabin for something he had forgotten.

Jimmy went on splitting wood, but he knew where Burkey was every second.

It happened swiftly. As Burkey came out of the cabin and headed back down to the *Alyce,* he glanced to determine Jimmy's whereabouts and did not see the puddle of frozen dishwater just off the front stoop. The convict went down as though slapped by a giant hand; his leg cracked with the report of a rifle. He skidded half around and let out a bellow of pain.

Dropping his axe, Jimmy charged down the hill, keeping as much undergrowth between him and the man as possible to prevent Burkey from using his gun. Scampering across the beach, with one bound he sailed across the planks to the *Alyce;* with the next he was inside the tug with his hands on the old familiar controls. As he revved up the engine against the ice, he looked back. No need to worry. The man lay like a crumpled bird where he had fallen, helpless in pain.

Jimmy throttled down the engine and came back out on the afterdeck. A spatter of snowflakes fell, and the wind howled mournfully. Over the headland, he could hear Lake Superior working herself into a heavy sea.

The convict could see him on the deck of the Alyce, knew that the boy had won back his freedom, but he made no move to call out. Jimmy realized that the man knew that he would die without help but was too proud to ask.

Jimmy shivered as much from the excitement of being free as from the freezing cold. Maybe with Burkey's leg broken, he could handle him safely, set the leg in splints in the warm shelter of the cabin, then, when Lake Superior had calmed a bit with evening, leave Burkey on his bed, push out past the shoals, and hightail it to Michipicoten Harbor to summon help. At any rate, he couldn't just leave the man to die there in the cold.

He shut off the engine and moved back to the afterdeck.

"You!" he commanded. "Throw the gun down the hill!"

For a moment he thought Burkey hadn't heard, then he saw the man fumble under his coat and send the pistol spinning down the frozen hillside, where Jimmy retrieved it, checked it for ammunition, and put it in his belt.

Propping himself up, Burkey took out his knife and slit his trouser leg down one side, exposing a swollen and discolored leg. The man's teeth were chattering, and he was pale with shock.

Jimmy was still too wary to come close. He cut Burkey a crutch from a mountain ash thicket and slid it to him. "Get in the cabin," he ordered, "and lie down. I'll cut some splints and build up a big fire in the stove."

The boy had no idea what splints looked like, but he figured anything that would help immobilize the leg would do.

Silent in his agony, Burkey pulled himself up on the single crutch, and with his useless leg swinging, hobbled slowly to the cabin.

Jimmy followed, pistol in hand, keeping his distance as the convict moved to his bed, lying back with his bad leg over the edge. Still not daring to turn his back on Burkey, Jimmy put wood on the fire and opened the drafts on the stove, then put on a pot of water for tea.

With Burkey lying silent, as if in a coma, the boy tiptoed out the door, closing it quietly behind him. Outside, he picked up a splitting maul and an axe, then headed for the spruce thicket behind the cabin. Selecting a dry, seasoned tree, he felled it, cut several three-foot lengths, and split them into staves with the maul.

When he came around the corner of the cabin with the splints, he saw that the cabin door was open, and Burkey was halfway down the hill toward the *Alyce.*

"Stop where you are!" Jimmy shouted, brandishing the revolver.

It was as though Burkey were deaf or out of his head. He lurched down the hill, hopping on his good leg, pushing with his crutch. In a moment he would be aboard.

Three times, Jimmy fired over the man's head, but still he hobbled on.

The convict had just started out over the slippery planks to the deck when suddenly his strength seemed to fail. He sagged and went down, body poised over the water. For a moment his eyes opened and he looked at Jimmy. "You win, Kid. Better take your old tub and go. And hurry. Couple more hours, and you won't have a chance against the weather."

"I'll get you to the cabin first," Jimmy said. "But no more tricks."

"I'll make it," Burkey said. "Get the hell out, Kid. Now!"

It was a decision the boy didn't want to have to make. It wasn't the violence of Lake Superior that frightened him, it was leaving his enemy to die. Before he could get back to the island with help, the convict would be dead. He sagged against a beached log and sat down on it. All the tensions of the past months caught up with him, and for the first time since his mother died three years before, Jimmy started to cry.

The hot tears scalded his face. "Mom! Mom!" he cried to the winds. "Help me! I don't know what to do, Mom! I guess I'm still just a kid. Help me make up my mind!"

Burkey's cheeks were waxen now with shock. A terrible spasm of shivering seized his large body. For a moment the boy considered taking the man on board the *Alyce* and making a run for civilization, but what Burkey needed was lots of heat, and the stove on the *Alyce* wasn't that great. Burkey's only real chance lay in getting up the slope again to the warm cabin.

Jimmy lay a tarp on the ground and rolled the inert body upon it, then tied a rope on one end and skidded his cargo across the frozen ground. He did not stop for rest until he had his enemy laid out on the floor of the cabin and had slammed the door against the cold.

No need to hurry now. He covered the convict

with blankets, then set about tearing strips of bedsheet, tying splints to immobilize the broken leg.

Once the wind blew open the rectory door and showered them with snow, but he shouldered it closed and barricaded it with the heavy table. He had gotten the man indoors none too soon. Outside the first major storm of winter was roaring down from Hudson Bay.

Jimmy spent the night without much sleep, tending his captor, listening fearfully to the wind howling like wolves about the eaves and the muffled thump of snow falling from heavily laden boughs. Once he shone his lantern out the window as though to check on the *Alyce,* but the beam vanished in a swirl of blown snow, and he moved to add wood to the stove, glad that Burkey had built the cabin strong and snug.

He was not afraid of the convict now; the man could not survive without his help. He climbed up into the rafters and hid the pistol so that Burkey could not steal it as he slept.

fourteen

AS THE DAYS PASSED, Riggs Burkey grew no better, but took spells of ranting and raving in delirium. Jimmy had little choice but to keep the cabin uncomfortably hot and to spoon feed his enemy with nourishing soups and tea. The leg swelled to twice its normal size and must have hurt the man a great deal. But even when Jimmy removed the splints and bathed the leg in hot water, he never flinched. At times he opened his eyes and followed the boy's movements around the room, but he seemed to have little recognition either of his whereabouts or his predicament. There was no way he could be left alone.

In the cold snap after the storm, ice froze quickly. Jimmy chopped the *Alyce* free from its grip, then using the powerful anchor winch deadmanned to a huge tree, managed to slide the *Alyce* up a set of iced skids, so that the winter ice would not damage her planking. She lay on her side as awkward and out of place as a beached whale, but safe.

One afternoon, while Jimmy was changing the dressings on Burkey's leg, the sun came through the gloomy winter overcast and bathed the snowbound forest in purest light, streaming through the front windows of the cabin to dapple and play on the multihued linoleum. Jimmy heard noises outside the cabin and looked out to see a pair of gray jays, loose and shaggy in winter overcoats, tugging at some leftover hotcakes he had tossed out onto the snow.

Jimmy chuckled, and Burkey opened his eyes at the sound. "Hey," the boy said. "You ought to see what's out there!" He reached under Burkey's pillow and pulled out the field guide, turned to an illustration of a Canada jay, and held it up for the man to see.

For a long time the sick convict stared, trying to focus his eyes; Jimmy thought he saw the faintest gleam of recognition and the tiniest hint of a smile. Then the eyes closed again, and regular breathing showed that the man slept.

The next day, for the first time, Burkey appeared better. It was as though he had suddenly decided to live. That afternoon, as Jimmy came tramping into the cabin from a snowshoe trip to the north end of the island, he saw that the man had opened the field guide by himself and turned to the Canada jays.

"You, Kid. C'mere."

He summoned Jimmy to his bedside. A look almost of embarrassment crossed Burkey's face. Pointing to the two words under the illustration, he tapped first one and then the other, and said, carefully,

"Canada——jay" then looked over for confirmation.

"Yeah," Jimmy said. "Canada jay." He glanced at the convict, suddenly curious. "Hey," he blurted out. "You can't even read!" Instantly he was sorry he had said it.

But Burkey managed a thin smile. "Never learned," he admitted. Then he peered up and said hesitantly, as he tapped the book. "Can you teach me to read this?"

"Teach you?" Jimmy said, startled at the very idea. "Teach you from a bird book? I dunno. Never tried to teach anyone anything before." He looked down to see disappointment in the man's eyes and realized what a hard thing it had been for Burkey to swallow his pride and ask.

"Yeah," he said to his captor. "I guess it'd be sort of fun."

His face flushed with embarrassment, the boy went to a window to look out. In a mountain ash tree just outside the cabin, a whole flock of pine grosbeaks was working the frozen orange berries with large black beaks. The females were washed with yellow, but the males were big fluffy bundles of pink, the colors made even more dramatic by the background of white snow.

"Hey, Man," Jimmy said. "Would you lookit out there! Pine grosbeaks! Must be a hunnerd of 'em. You want to see? I'll move your bed."

Inhabitants of the far north, the big, gentle birds had never learned to fear Man. They looked up only briefly at the sounds of Burkey's bed scuffing across the floor, and the sudden fluttering of the flour-sack curtains as Jimmy eased them aside and tied them so the man could see out.

Burkey stared in amazement at the grosbeaks; in the north country there are few sights more spectacular. Carefully, page by page, he went through the field guide until he found their picture. A sudden shy smile showed above his beard, and he pointed to the inscription, tracing it with a clumsy forefinger. "Pine," he said slowly and proudly. "Pine—gros—beak!"

"Hey," Jimmy said, "that's just great! You're getting it, even if it is a screwy way to learn how to read."

fifteen

THE NEXT MORNING when Jimmy came stomping in out of the snow, he found Burkey in a rage. From the looks of the blankets, he had tried to get himself up and perhaps for the first time realized his helplessness and total dependence upon the boy. He glared at Jimmy as though the whole situation were his fault.

The leg looked swollen and angry, needing care, but when Jimmy set the water on the stove to boil and added balsam needles to make a poultice, Burkey waved him away.

"I don't need help," he snarled. He tried to pull himself up but fell back, and his face turned gray with pain. For some minutes he lay with eyes closed, as Jimmy fanned the big stove to cooking heat and started breakfast.

He sliced some bacon from a frozen slab and put it on the griddle to fry, then mixed powdered eggs, dried milk, and water into an omelette. The fragrance filled the cabin, but when the boy set a plate of blueberry muffins, honey, bacon, and eggs beside the man's bed, Burkey did not open his eyes.

When Jimmy had finished his own breakfast, he put on his coat and left Burkey alone. Strolling down to the harbor, enjoying the squeak of hard snow under his feet, he examined the *Alyce*. Beneath her load of snow, the old tug looked like a huge white mushroom. Afraid that the weight of the heavy pack might do damage to the cabin, he took a shovel and worked at carving blocks of snow, tumbling them down to the surface of the pack covering the harbor. When the chore was done, he cleaned the deck and managed to open the door of the cabin.

The room had a dank, silent chill about it that sank through his coat. He crawled over the slanting floor to the wheel, caressing the grips, wishing he could start the engine and move out to sea, to freedom.

Christmas must be coming up soon, and he didn't even know the days. He pictured some of his pals in school. Even if he went back tomorrow, there was no way now he could catch up. He'd be forever behind them. One day they'd all be going to the senior prom, even graduating, and he'd still be a junior. Since the day of the accident, he had avoided tears, but now two big drops coursed down his cheeks, spattered on the floor, and swiftly froze. Out of water, the *Alyce* seemed no longer a boat, alive, rising and falling with the swells, but a rock, part of Mother Earth herself.

Outside the cabin, as he stood on the deck, the air seemed almost warm to him. A flock of cedar waxwings, holding each other in formation with soft calls, rising and falling with each wingbeat as they flew, passed high overhead, circling the island as though scouting for remnant berries.

The crust on the snow was like iron, enabling him to move easily through the frozen forest. From somewhere far off, toward the north end of the island, he heard riflelike shots, but when he listened carefully, he realized it was only trees exploding in the cold. Walking along the headland, he looked out over Lake Superior, now locked flat and waveless, a white, featureless plain stretching to the gray of the horizon.

He was glad to move back from the cliffs to the sheltered beauty of the inner forest. A pair of Canada jays followed him along, hoping for a tidbit, and he was glad of their company.

Through a patch of clear, windblown ice on one of the lakes, he saw a beaver pass beneath his feet, pushing a slender birch branch, leaving a trail of bubbles. He found the house, but it was only a huge mound of snow. In the warm, moist chamber, the mother beaver would be placidly awaiting the time of birth, safe from her enemies, the lynx that sometimes crossed over the ice pack, or the otters, which had a snow slide at the far end of the dam.

In the coniferous thickets at the northern edge of the island, he saw a spruce grouse; it flew up on a nearby branch and eyed him. He could have killed it with a stick and feasted that night on its thick, juicy breast meat, but he passed it by, pretending not to see.

Crossing over an esker into another drainage, he paused to rest in a thicket of white birch and mountain ash. The snow beneath the trees was orange with fallen berries where hosts of birds had been stripping the fruit from the branches. Tiny birch seeds winged away from the parent tree with each passing breeze.

Here on this frozen bit of real estate in the middle of Lake Superior, a host of species had learned to survive. A piece of bark hit the boy squarely on the head, and he looked up to see the flashing golden crown of a black-backed three-toed woodpecker.

"Hey," Jimmy said, grinning up at the bird, "you cut that out!"

The woodpecker moved to the other side of the bole, but peered around it occasionally to better observe this interloper in its forest.

A convocation of feathered upside-downers came flitting through the thicket. Chickadees, nuthatches, brown creepers, and kinglets, all searching for tiny egg cases beneath the loose bark scrolls of the birches.

A fragment of a poem lost forever with his mother's death teased his memory:

> It wasn't snow kept me so late
> I made the teacher frown.
> I stopped to watch some chickadees
> All feeding upside down.

"Mine! Mine!" a blue jay screamed from the stub of a dying spruce, jolting Jimmy out of memories; but the bird gave up the territory easily enough to a great black-and-white snowy owl that floated up to usurp the perch and regarded the clamor it was causing in the understory below with innocent yellow eyes.

There were no mice on the island or squirrels, and Jimmy wondered what this migrant from the far reaches of Canada could possibly find to eat. Moments later, the huge owl gave up on the island and beat its way silently southward. As long as he flew against a backdrop of spruce, Jimmy saw him well; but as soon as the owl rose against the leaden skies, he was immediately gone. He would rest somewhere out on the ice pack, all but invisible on the snow, making short journeys until he reached the Michigan coast. There he would hunt the open fields until spring drove him north again.

As he skirted the bluffs on the west side of the island, Jimmy happened to glance out over the ice toward Ontario and saw a herd of twenty woodland caribou, drifting single-file over the ice toward his island. From his vantage point on the cliffs, he could see four far-off specks behind them, gray shadows of timber wolves, following patiently enough, waiting perhaps for some mishap to one of the herd.

At other seasons the cliffs would have prevented the caribou from gaining the island except across that path of ice where the harbor joined Lake Superior;

but on this western shore, the snow driven by winter gales had ramped up over the cliffs into the timber. It was up one of these huge snow ridges that the caribou passed onto the island and were lost in the forests.

The wolves lay patiently at a distance out on the ice as though waiting for dusk before they went ashore. Jimmy knew the wolves were like ghosts in the forest and would not harm a man, but just the same he felt small and vulnerable. When he moved inland, circling the caribou so as not to alarm them, the wolves were still lying nose to tail, asleep on the ice.

When he returned to the cabin, he found that Burkey had propped himself up against pillows and was looking at the bird book. He had obviously been matching birds he knew with the words that identified them. Now he beckoned Jimmy to his bedside and opened the book to a page marked with a turned-down corner. "Look here, Kid," he said with excitement. "There was one of these settin' in the mountain ash."

He ran his finger tip along the name. "Var—" he pronounced carefully.

"Var—what?" Jimmy coached, glad to see the man in a better mood.

"Varlet."

"You're guessing. Try again."

"Varied!"

"Good!" Jimmy said. "Now varied what?"

"Varied thr-ush."

"Varied thrush!" Jimmy said. "You were lucky. I have yet to see one on the island."

"Here, Kid," Burkey said, pointing to the text beneath the illustration. "Read me what it says."

"Read it yourself," Jimmy replied. He pointed to the first word, and the man concentrated hard, his forehead wrinkling into a frown.

"A," he said. "A north-ern?"

"Good," Jimmy said.

"A northern nester?"

"Right on."

It was beginning to get dark in the cabin when Burkey finished laboring over the paragraph. Jimmy took down one of the Coleman lamps, filled it with white gasoline, pumped up the base with air, replaced the broken mantles and allowed them to burn to ash, then lit it. The cabin was suddenly cheery with yellow light.

Jimmy cooked a good supper of potatoes, dried salmon in cream, and canned peas. For once the man ate heartily, cleaning up his plate. Some of the swelling on his leg had gone down, and for the first time, the discoloration looked less angry.

Tired from his long walk in the snow, Jimmy had barely finished the dishes and leaned back comfortably in a chair before he dozed off. When he awakened fitfully a few hours later, the lamp still shone brightly in the cabin, and the big man still pored over the bird book, mouthing his words silently as he studied his lesson.

sixteen

JIMMY HAD A FEELING that Christmas might have come and gone without him knowing and that it might even be a new year. Often, as he took his daily hike through the forest, he tried to remember a Munising resplendent with Christmas lights and to remember the fun of pulling a laden toboggan over crisp, moonlit snow to deliver gifts to friends. You had a family big as the whole town, you had to limit your list. He figured he had a pretty good touch in sensing those who needed a lift. If there was a joy in giving, there was also a joy in being remembered, no matter how small the gift.

Perhaps, on the island, he would have bypassed Christmas altogether had not a spruce grouse flown against a cabin window and fluttered crazynecked and dying on the snow. It was as though Providence had provided them with a Christmas turkey. Within moments, Jimmy had his knife out and had made an incision in the abdomen.

Despite the cold, he worked carefully, for he had plans for the delicate plumage. Gently, so as not to tear the skin, he worked it free of the leg bones, then cut through the tail, slipping the skin up over the back as though it were a sweater two sizes too large.

Once he had salted the skin and dried it, Jimmy stripped wolf moss from the trees, took string from a drawer in the *Alyce,* and began modeling a reproduction of the body he had just removed. Tying string around a ball of moss, he began winding, adding moss here and there until every bulge in the original body had been duplicated. Inserting wires for the legs, wings, neck, and tail, he pulled the skin carefully over the moss, inserting the wires through the hollow bones, then sewing up the abdomen.

Mounting the grouse in a lifelike position on a slab of bark, he preened the bird's feathers with a twig. The resulting figure was a trifle lopsided and comical, but unmistakably a spruce grouse. Jimmy managed a grin of satisfaction.

When Burkey awoke from a nap, there was a Christmas tree on the floor of the cabin, a grouse cooking in the oven, a package on his bed tied with strips of colored cloth, a fat pillow stuffed with fragrant balsam fir needles, and a wreath of fir cones hung on the inside of the rectory door.

The convict looked about the cabin in wonder, then turned his face away. Jimmy approached his bed. When Burkey looked at him, he thought the man's eyes were no longer hard and suspicious.

Jimmy pushed forward the package containing the spruce grouse. "Merry Christmas," he said.

Burkey stared at the package as though reluctant to accept a gift. Gingerly, he took off the wrapping and smiled.

"Spruce grouse," he recited. "A large, rather tame grouse of northern coniferous forests, sometimes referred to as a 'fool hen.'"

"Hey!" Jimmy chuckled. "That's all right! You've been reading some yourself."

"I didn't tell you," the man said. "There's been one feeding on berries around the cabin. I saw it in the mountain ash and looked it up. Took me a while, but I managed to read up on it."

The boy nodded toward the stuffed bird. "Most likely this is the one you saw. Flew into the cabin window. The rest of it is in the oven. We'll just pretend it's turkey."

Burkey fumbled beneath his pillow and brought out a wooden carving. "This here's for you," he said abruptly, handing it to the boy.

It was Jimmy's turn to be surprised. Burkey had carved a beautiful pine grosbeak out of wood. Feather perfect, except for a lack of color, it looked almost real. The man had talent!

"Never tried a bird before," he said. "Cellmate of mine in the pen at Marquette taught me how to handle a knife. A carving knife that is. The two of us carved horses and knickknacks to sell in the prison store."

"Where did this wood come from?" Jimmy marveled.

"Just a piece of oak that split off the far side of the bedstead," Burkey said. "Then I whittled off everything that didn't look like a pine grosbeak. The shavings I hid under the bed." He glanced at the bird resting in Jimmy's hand. "Paint," he said. "What it needs is a bit of paint. Saw some in your boat. Bunch of half empty cans in a cupboard next to the engine, but I couldn't get down there to get them. Had some red and some gray to rub into the grain, I could make that grosbeak sing!"

Jimmy took the grouse out of the oven and served it with cranberry sauce, reconstituted potatoes, and biscuits. Wintering as it had on spruce needles, the grouse tasted heavily of turpentine, but they ate every morsel, picking the carcass clean.

They had hardly finished supper when from somewhere in the forest north of the cabin they heard a long melodious howl, joined in harmony by another and yet another singer.

"What's that?" Burkey hissed, turning pale.

"Wolves," Jimmy answered. "Saw twenty caribou out on the ice on Lake Superior. They found a place where the snow had ramped up over the cliffs on the windward side and, with their big snowshow hooves, made it up on the island. There were four wolves following them but keeping their distance."

For a long time the convict listened to the wild music. Only when it ceased did he take up his book, leaning back on the balsam pillow Jimmy had made, to mouth words silently to himself.

Whenever he had trouble, he would consult the boy.

"C'mere a minute, Kid," he said as Jimmy finished the dishes. "Either I'm reading this book wrong or this Pough feller that wrote it is some liar."

He pointed to a section he was laboring over on the pileated woodpecker. "The book claims this here woodpecker is eighteen inches long and makes rectangular holes in trees instead of round. Now I can't swallow that!"

"He's right, though," Jimmy said. "There's a pair here on the island. I heard one calling yesterday from a stand of big timber on the east side. And they do make rectangular holes. You think a pileated is strange, today I saw a woodpecker that has only three toes on a foot instead of four."

As the man took up the book and went on reading, Jimmy moved to his side and began bathing the broken leg with warm water from a pot of balsam needles, noting that the swelling was down and the color less angry. There had to be magic in that brew. By spring, Burkey should be out and around, able to fend for himself, and Jimmy could once more look for a chance to escape.

seventeen

THE NEXT MORNING, Jimmy searched the neighboring forest for seasoned white pine, cutting into several dead snags before he found one with interesting patterns in the grain. He felled the tree on the snow, cut off a block, and packed it to the cabin. The sick man's eyes lit up when he saw it.

"There's a loon in that block," he said. "I can see it. Watch me make it come alive!"

When he took up his tools, it was as though nothing in the room but the block of wood existed for him.

Leaving Burkey to his work, Jimmy went off through the forest, hoping for a better look at the caribou. The crust was frozen hard, which made traveling without snowshoes easy, but each step broadcast his presence to any wild things that might be listening.

Not far from camp, he picked up the trail of four wolves and followed them, reading every sign. They had caught up to the caribou bedded down on a knoll, put them to flight, then isolated one of the weaker animals on a rocky cliff above Lake Superior. From the tracks, the animal had had two choices: to run for it and die, or to leap and die. The cow had chosen to leap; or perhaps, as she had backed up to the edge of the cliff against the onslaught, the snow had given way beneath her hind legs and she had toppled to the ice below. The wolves had traveled some distance down the island's edge before a drift had allowed them to descend to the ice. Now only puffs of hair, a few cracked bone fragments, and dark stains on the ice pack, marked the end of the drama.

Once as Jimmy retraced his own trail, he saw that the wolves had been following him through the thickets. He smiled to himself, knowing that this was only a sign of their curiosity and that confronted by his presence, they would vanish. They were the veterinarians of the forest. Once the weak and unfit caribou, heavily infested with parasites, were weeded from the herd, they would drift on, looking for easier picking.

Near the north end of the island, the caribou had watched for a time from a thicket, then moved on, feeding as they went. They had filtered through a heavy spruce wood, grazing on mosses and lichens, their large, semicircular hooves holding them up like snowshoes even when there was no crust.

Somewhere ahead of him, Jimmy heard an animal cough. A twig snapped, and he heard the slow squeak of hooves on frozen snow. Glimpsing dark shadows moving toward him, he dropped quickly behind a long ridge of snow that marked the grave of a fallen tree. The caribou were feeding directly toward him.

In the distance, a wolf howled, and a giant bull caribou raised his antlers from the brush and listened, gauging distance and intent, then went on browsing unconcerned. A cow and weanling calf moved to the edge of the clearing. Here the yearling made a half-hearted attempt to nurse, but his mother lowered her head and shook her small horns at him, then moved off to investigate the tip of a highbush huckleberry protruding from the snow. The bull moved up to forage beside her, wraithes of steam rising from his nostrils in the bitter cold.

Restlessly, the herd drifted on. In the rear, an old dry cow moved listlessly, her coat drab and lifeless, her hips spattered with raven droppings, as though the birds had marked her for slaughter, perching on her back waiting for the parasites gnawing on her bowels to do their inevitable damage. Jimmy sensed that soon the wolves trailing the herd would come upon her and show her the final mercy. Cruel as it might seem, such a death was swift and better than a long, slow lingering.

As he lay, the cold soon seeped through his clothing, and he knew that he had better be up and moving. Not wanting to alarm the caribou, he set off directly away from them, then cut southward across a frozen lake bed. A huge flock of snow buntings wheeled and circled over the snow expanse, flying as though leaderless, as though each of the thousand birds making up the flock were but a single cell of a whole. Yet let one bird along the edge turn from the flock, and instantly the rest made it leader.

Unafraid, they landed almost at Jimmy's feet, hopping about in search of winged seeds of pine, spruce, fir, or birch, blown out over the snow. Bodies snowdrift white, marked with fawn, they were hard to see. Jimmy stood stock still, enjoying their trusting ways, relishing their company, until the flock became restive to be on, and the air was suddenly noisy with flutter of wings and twittering calls. The flock circled, flashing in the air, awaiting a leader, flowing across the snowfields, until a vanguard formed around one bird and dropped to feed along the far shore of a pond, and the rest funneled after.

It was almost dusk when Jimmy returned to the cabin, glad enough to seek the warmth of the stove. He brought Burkey a snow bunting feather and listened patiently as the man found the illustration in the field guide and labored over the text.

The man's day had been well spent. His bed was a mass of wood shavings, and the blankets needed a good shaking out of doors. The block of white pine had been roughed into the shape of a loon. Tomorrow and each day after, the shavings would become finer as the man carved and scraped, until the loon was feather perfect and the wood glowed with the body and spirit of every loon that ever sailed the northland.

Burkey seemed glad enough to put down his work and listen as Jimmy recounted his day: finding the last vestiges of the caribou on the ice, the birds he'd seen, the woodland caribou as they fed near him through the thickets at the north end. He questioned the boy about the buntings, how they had sounded, what they had been feeding on, whether males and females traveled in the same flock. It was as though the book had only whetted his curiosity and he thirsted to know more.

The next day a series of wild storms swept across Lake Superior, engulfing the tiny cabin in snow, which blew in wave after wave across the ice-bound lake. Drifting up through the forest, it piled about the windows until only the Coleman lamp gave them light.

The snow drifted then to the eaves and up over the roof, until a traveler would have been hard put to find the outline of the cabin under the massive dunes of white. Jimmy was glad now that Burkey had insisted on strong rafters, for above their heads the roof creaked ominously under its growing load.

As Jimmy attempted to go out for firewood, he found that the weight of snow on the logs had jammed the heavy door, making it impossible to open. He managed to slide up a window, and, by cutting blocks of snow and melting them on the stove for water, he was finally able to tunnel to the woodpile.

Insulated by the growing snowpack, the cabin became stifling hot. Leaking through the roof around the flashing, meltwater trickled down the stovepipe before vanishing in a puff of steam. There were few other sounds: the hissing of the Coleman lamp, the scraping of Burkey's knife, the ticking of the stove as it heated or cooled, and the far off moan of blizzard winds fluting in the stovepipe. It was as though the world outside had ceased to exist.

"I think some of that snow piled outside has blown in clear from Duluth," Jimmy remarked.

Burkey looked up from his work and nodded. "In this gale there can't be much left out on the lake. If I'd been smarter, I would have built a snow fence of brush downslope from the cabin to divert the snow past us. The way the trees around the cabin are all gnarled and broken, I reckon snow drifts in heavily like this every winter."

The rafters were beginning to bow under the load and creaked ominously. Burkey cursed his helplessness, and the passing hours only increased their sense of being trapped. "You've got to fight your way out," Burkey said, "and have a look around."

"If I do get out," Jimmy replied, "what if I take the saw with me and fell a tree or two to windward? That would leave us under the lee, with the wind sweeping by on either side."

Falling from the ceiling, a drop of meltwater struck the hot shade of the lamp, and the flowered glass shattered musically and crumpled in jagged shards around the gleaming brass base. The fragile mantles of silk ash trembled but they did not break.

Putting Burkey's coat over his own, Jimmy tossed a shovel out the window, then saw and snowshoes.

"At the end of the woodpile," Burkey advised, "there's a good-sized spruce. Might be you could force your way up through the branches."

Jimmy stood on the end of the woodpile and tried his best, but the branches anchored the snow and made an impenetrable barrier. He tried compacting the snow with his head, but the snow gave only so much and turned to ice under the pressure.

The roof seemed the answer. Standing on the ramp of the woodpile, he slowly cut out blocks with the shovel, keeping close to the cabin wall, until at last, he turned the corner over the eaves, and the dim light from the cabin no longer followed him.

Twice the tunnel collapsed behind him; fearful of suffocating, he kicked his way back down the slippery tube. In the comfort of the lamplight he lay resting, heart pounding, until he had composed himself and built up courage to try again.

Foot by foot, he tunneled along the rising roof, careful to keep above the gables where the structure was strongest.

At last, above his head, the snowpack let in a gleam of light, and with a great heave, he broke through into a howl of wind. Screening his face with his mittens, he took a quick look about. It was still snowing hard. Driven by fierce winds, the snow whirled across the flats, traveling in an endless stream toward the timber, to be caught and held at last by the thick forest about the cabin.

The wind sucked his breath away, and he retreated for the moment into his burrow. Then, when he had warmed a bit, he managed a look down slope toward the two spruces that were his quarry. He was right! The trees lay in the path of the wind. Felled one on the other, they might divert enough snow to one side or another to make a difference.

Retreating once more into his lair, he rested for a moment, then pushed saw and snowshoes ahead of him out the end of the tunnel. Pulling a scarf over his face until only his eyes showed, he rolled out onto the snowshoes, careful not to step off into the deep powder. Strapping them on, he took his saw and headed toward the trees. As he passed near the top of the stovepipe, he saw that it was completely buried, and smoke rose from a dirty black volcano in the drift.

The bow saw was not made for heavy work, and he was forced to saw slowly, carefully, for fear the blade would shatter in the cold. His mittens froze to the metal handle, and his fingers grew numb, but he worked on, sawing out a kerf in the direction he wanted the tree to fall. Once the kerf flopped out onto the snow, he moved to the back side of the tree, arching his back against the wind. He had made only a few strokes with the saw when the wind did the rest, shoving over the tree with a splintering crash.

Jimmy beat his mittens against his chest to try to restore circulation, then tackled the second tree. Moments later it fell across the first, and quickly the snow began to accumulate among the branches. When Jimmy saw the first streams of snow deflect away from the cabin area, he hurried back up the hillside, kicked off his snowshoes, and dove like a rabbit into his burrow.

eighteen

THE STORM THAT BURIED the cabin was followed by several weeks of such bitter cold that both Burkey and Jimmy were glad of the sheath of snow about them. Where once the heavy pack had been a threat to their lives, now it insulated them from sub-zero temperatures made even more lethal by near constant winds.

Birds clustered around the cabin stovepipe for warmth, and on Jimmy's few excursions on snowshoes away from the cabin, he found jays, chickadees, brown creepers, and nuthatches frozen to death in the snow. He set out feeding stations across the island and kept them stocked with biscuits, hoping that this might help them survive.

Once as he moved through a thicket on his errands of mercy, he came upon the wolves, faces hoary with frost, laying huddled, nose to tail beside a caribou carcass. Half buried in fluffy snow, they seemed reluctant to flee, and simply eyed him curiously as he hurried past.

There had been twenty caribou when they arrived on the island; now as he saw them standing along the shore of a frozen lake, slab sides turned toward the weak northern sun, he counted only sixteen.

Used to confinement, Burkey seemed content within the confines of the cabin. While Jimmy restlessly braved the cold to cut firewood and sled it back to the cabin, the man spent hours poring over the bird book and learning how to write. Jimmy showed him the alphabet as he himself had learned to write it, but the man would have none of such a careless scrawl. Soon he developed his own no-nonsense meticulous style; painstakingly, he copied every word of the field guide into his own handwriting.

When Jimmy found a bird frozen in the snow, he brought it back with him, cradling it carefully so as not to muss a feather. First Burkey carved it in wood, imitating its colors as closely as the limited selection of paints from the *Alyce* would allow. Once he had captured the bird in wood, feather perfect, he carefully skinned it, salted it down, then packed the specimen with dry moss. Every day the intense cold added different specimens to his collection.

He had committed Pough's field guide to memory, and no longer was it necessary for Jimmy to identify new species. Rather it was Jimmy who sometimes had to consult the convict.

It was the loons, above all other species, that the man seemed to find most fascinating. If Jimmy had found Burkey a silent companion on those canoe trips the summer before, he realized now that his captor had been absorbed in a world totally new to him. When it came to loons, Burkey could describe in detail every action, every call, every defense posture, every idiosyncrasy of every loon he'd seen. And when Jimmy explained that loons were becoming rare due to harassment by sporting boats, human population pressures, and pollution such as acid rain, he took his island as being the loon capitol of the world; he worried over each pair as though he had perhaps seen them for the last time.

"Hey, Man," Jimmy said once, coming in from the snow as Burkey pored over his bird skins. "If you'd started that as a kid, you might a become the best bird scientist in the whole world."

Burkey glanced at him quietly, and the boy had a feeling that rather than resent what the past years had dealt him, Riggs Burkey thought only of catching up with what he had missed.

Burkey's leg had not healed straight and must still pain him a great deal, but he forced himself off his bed and exercised the now-shrunken muscles. Like a caged animal he paced back and forth on the crutches Jimmy cut for him, swinging the near useless leg on before.

One mild day toward the end of winter, Jimmy went out on snowshoes; he was just skirting the rotting ice on one of the lakes, when he saw the wolf pack on ahead, working the little band of caribou.

The wolves seemed determined to keep the caribou milling about, for every time the herd would move ahead, a wolf would break from cover and turn them back. Time and again, the caribou tried a half-hearted break in one direction or another, but the wolves seemed to anticipate them, thwarting their escape. Four wolves seemed like a dozen.

One of the wolves was an old female heavy with pups. It may have been that being pregnant she was less than agile, for as the caribou rushed her way, she rose from behind a snowdrift in their path and, head lowered, blocked their advance.

Perhaps the caribou sensed her clumsiness, or were tired of games, for they decided to run on past her. As she snarled and attempted to block their path, she slipped and went down, and the herd thundered over the top of her.

When she struggled to her feet, Jimmy saw that she was limping badly and was hardly able to drag herself into the timber. One big wolf went to her and briefly touched his nose to her muzzle, then was off with the rest in pursuit of the herd.

Some time later, as Jimmy was working his way along the cliffs, hoping to see some signs of a disintegrating ice pack, he saw the caribou out on Lake Superior, headed in the direction of Michipicoten Island. Some distance behind the herd, three wolves trailed along patiently, biding their time. Curious about the wounded female, Jimmy tried to track her, but soon lost all sign of her in the dense thickets.

Without caribou to feed on, and no rodents except beaver on the island, he had to assume that the injured wolf would have a hard time. The next day, the first in a series of chinook winds blew in off Lake Superior, raising havoc with the snow pack, and he forgot her in his excitement. Spring had finally arrived!

nineteen

JIMMY DUG OUT THE FRONT DOOR of the cabin, cleared a place along the south wall, and set a block of pine close beside, so that Burkey could sit leaning back against the warm logs to sun himself. Jimmy was freckled and ruddy from windburn and glare of sun on snow, but the man, beneath his tousled red-black beard, was the pale ivory of a plant growing beneath a rock.

When Burkey was not hobbling back and forth, exercising his leg, he made the seat his headquarters; and there, binoculars ready, he watched for the first migrating birds heading north. Jimmy could sense the man's quiet excitement as he waited for the new arrivals.

One day the lakes on the island were mere fields of white snow, the next they had turned to brown slush as each watercourse joined its downstream neighbor and rushed on, spilling over the long series of mud and stick beaver dams until they poured their coffee into Lake Superior.

Lying high and dry during the winter, beached on her side, the *Alyce* rose with the torrent and righted herself, tugging at her anchor chain as though impatient to be underway. Great cakes of froth from upland waterfalls sailed the currents, often splitting on *Alyce*'s bow before swirling past the harbor entrance into the big lake where they piled against the stubborn ice pack.

The waterfowl came first. Old squaw ducks with elegant pointed tails and clarion calls. White-winged scoters flapping the new water into a froth, setting up a community yodel. Somber scaups and black ducks, elegant black-and-white buffleheads and golden-eye. Then came great whistling swans, white as snowdrifts, resting up on a journey that would take them north toward Hudson Bay and beyond.

Eventually the first pair of loons flew in over the ice packs of Lake Superior and circled the island, uttering the high-pitched tremolo one hears only in flight, then settled quickly on the lake that had been their personal fiefdom the summer before, staking their claim as though they knew they were vanguard to a host of other loons arriving an hour or so later.

Soon every pond, every lake, every waterway on the island that would support loons echoed and re-echoed with eerie wails as family after family joined in the chorus. It seemed to Jimmy that the sound spread from one loon family to another until all the loons in the north were in chorus.

As though feeling left out, the white-winged scoters set up a chorus of their own, and the swans whooped and beat their strong white wings, then settled back to sip the waters.

Off shore, the ice pack gave in to the assault. On the windward side of the island, ice drove ashore in shards, piling fifty feet high, while on the leeward side, a long, mirror-calm lake developed between the towering red cliffs of the island and the retreating ice pack. To this long lake, herring gulls, loons, and mergansers flocked in numbers, feeding on a treasury of small fish that had been locked away by ice since freeze-up the fall before and now frolicked at the surface.

One morning as Jimmy walked a patch of bare ground looking for cowslips and spring beauties, he heard a strange whimpering coming from the jumble of sandstone slabs. It seemed to be the cry of a young animal lost or abandoned by its mother. Cautiously, the boy worked his way up the hillside until he could look into a small cavern formed of rubble fallen from a sandstone overhang.

As he climbed up over a rock, he froze in his tracks. There just ahead of him the injured wolf lay with her head on her paws watching him. Three of her cubs lay dead beside her; the fourth had wandered a short distance away and was gnawing hungrily on a piece of caribou hide. Now and then he would pause in his labors and let out a long plaintive whine as though his belly hurt from hunger.

It was as though the mother wolf had only kept herself alive until help arrived, for as Jimmy clutched the rock wall for support and sent a noisy shower of talus rattling down the slope, the great yellow eyes closed as in sleep, and a convulsive tremor seized her body. Moments later she was dead.

Sadly the boy ran his fingers through her soft underfur as a spring breeze rippled the black guard hairs along her ruff.

The pup was staring at him as though uncertain whether or not to flee into the rocky crevasses. Jimmy went on stroking the dead wolf, transferring the scent of the old female onto his own clothing. He whined his very best wolf whine, and when he glanced over at the pup, it had relaxed and was once more chewing on the hide.

For some time, Jimmy lay beside the body, until at last he felt a small wet nose touch his ear gingerly; then the pup climbed over his leg and crept between Jimmy and the dead wolf, nestling for warmth.

For some time the boy stroked the little animal, and called him soft names. When the cub seemed to accept such overtures, he slipped him quietly under his coat and, cradling him against his body, carried him back to camp.

Moments after his arrival, the weak, half-starved little wolfling was lapping happily away with both front feet in a bowl of reconstituted milk, while Burkey hovered over it like a great mother hen.

Perhaps it was his great beard, or a sense of quiet about the man that the pup liked, for he was Burkey's pal right from the start.

It was the convict who staggered up a dozen times during the night to warm his milk or caress the stains away with a soft damp cloth. It was the convict who played with him at wolf games, or slipped him choice morsels under the table at supper. It was the man he followed as Burkey made his first short expeditions into the forest in hopes of seeing new birds.

Sometimes when Jimmy came back to the cabin, he found the big man lying on the floor wrestling with the young animal as the wolf, mouth gaping wide, played at killing, going over the man's shoulder with a paw, and seizing his great mane with his jaws. Even as the pup grew, the relationship was such that Burkey trusted him. Mock killing was part of the wolf's play syndrome, and there was no malice to it.

Feeding the youngster was no problem for there were enough stores of dried protein to last the three of them for years. There were plenty of grouse on the island, and such wild meat for man or wolf would have been a welcome change; but somehow the winter had brought the two humans so close to the wildlife about them that such an act seemed unthinkable.

As the ice pack retreated and the last vestige of snow melted from southern exposures on the island, a great migration of warblers began; Burkey was beside himself with actually seeing birds he'd only read about. Migrants used the island as a stepping-stone across Lake Superior, and though Burkey had started his life bird list rather late, it grew daily by leaps and bounds.

He was a child in his wonder. Just as he came to understand that sandpipers nest along the shores of lakes and streams, laying eggs that resemble the pebbles lying about them, the man found a solitary sandpiper incubating her eggs in the abandoned abode of a robin, twenty feet up in a tree. Burkey found a cowbird's egg laid in a vireo's nest, by a parent too lazy to rear her own young; beneath a log he found the lopsided oven built by an oven bird, and under a waterfall spilling over the lip of a beaver dam, he discovered the bulky home of a water ouzel. The sight of a giant pileated woodpecker drilling a rectangular hole in a rotted log sent him back to the birdbook, hoping that there might be something on the pileated he had missed.

The loons had few unwatched moments. From vantage points in trees, or from hillsides above the small lakes, he spied on their courtship rites and marveled at their "shouting" matches as they defended territories against rivals. He heard every loon's voice as distinct from that of others, and remembered them.

Each male loon he named for a former cellmate. "That's Bird Dog," he'd say. "He lives on the pond by the cranberry bog. Right now he's sparring with Slick on the lake next door where all the pitcher plants grew last summer."

He kept well back from the bulky nests. "A nest is personal," he'd say. "They don't need me poking around. Might get the hen off her nest and a raven'd come a-flying to get the eggs, then it'd be on my conscience same as if I'd killed the baby birds myself."

"Conscience!" Jimmy scoffed. "What does he know

about a conscience? He can hold me prisoner and not worry about it, but he lays awake at night stewing about the chance that a raven or a sea gull will break a loon's egg. One of these days," Jimmy went on, "he'll drop his guard and make a mistake; he'll forget to take the keys to *Alyce,* and I'll be long gone. You can bet I'll make sure they lock him up and throw away the key!"

Yet down deep he knew that such resolutions were just so much wind in the poplar trees. One evening as he sat on a beaver dam and listened to the song of a northern waterthrush from a hidden perch in a black spruce, he realized that the rapture of the north had overcome him. He could plan escape after escape, but the scheme was always for 'after the loons hatch; after the wolf pup has grown some.' He found himself thinking of the little ship he'd launched the previous summer with a message that might, if found, cause Burkey's capture, even death. To be honest, he hoped the ship had been lost in a storm, and the message sent to the bottom of the Munising Trench.

twenty

JIMMY AND RIGGS BURKEY were watching a loon
hatch out her eggs from a hillside blind when the
wolf pup made its first kill. He had been sunning
himself, half-immersed in a bed of Clintonia and pink
lady slippers, when an unlucky spruce grouse sailed
across a clearing and landed a few feet from the pup.
Before the hapless bird could realize its mistake, the
wolf sprang, pinned it with his forefeet, and snapped
off its head.

For a moment the pup stood back timidly as the
grouse beat up a dust in one last reflexive burst of
wingbeats; then as his prize grew quiet, he caught
it up in his jaws, glancing down the hillside at his
human friends to see that they watched. But when
some vague suspicion seemed to enter his mind that
they might want to share, he carried the dead bird
to a secluded spot at the foot of a dead birch, where
he lay comfortably and devoured every scrap.

It was only when the last vestiges were gone, and
he had gone back to the source to see if there were

any more such windfalls about, that he trotted down to the blind and laid his head contentedly against Burkey's knee. The big man laid one ham of a hand on the wolf's ruff to acknowledge him, but went on watching loons.

Now that hatching was taking place, the male loon was especially protective of the nest. He cruised back and forth past a bulky island of marsh vegetation, like a gunboat protecting a harbor. Pity the harmless black duck or merganser that swam too near.

Once when the mother loon rocked back on her short legs to inspect the hatch, Burkey noted in his journal that one of the chicks had hatched completely, and the other had succeeded in pipping a trap door off the large end of the egg. By evening, the hen was still tight on her nest, but the heads of her two chicks had been seen surveying their new world from a vantage point among the feathers on her back.

Burkey spent the night in the blind; and, in the first faint light of dawn, awoke to find two chicks floating like puffs of cattail down on the mirror of the pond. The event was announced to the world by nervous parents, whose wails and tremolos were picked up by most of the other loons on the island.

Jimmy brought food to the blind, for Burkey would not leave the new family alone. Along the wetlands, mosquitoes and gnats still prospered, making the boy miserable. Burkey's hands, and those portions of his face not covered by beard, were soon raw with bites.

Now and then he swiped at the tormenting hordes half-heartedly, but his concentration was on the loons, or the myriad birds living along the shore of the lake.

Among the stores in the cache was a plentiful supply of insect repellent and some head nets, which helped make Jimmy's life more bearable. One day he persuaded Burkey to wear one of the nets; but when he returned, an hour later, it was cast aside over a bush, and the insects were back feasting. The device had come between Burkey and the loons, impairing his use of binoculars. Afraid to miss one little detail of loon behavior, he would have none of the net.

Much of what Burkey was discovering for himself seemed commonplace to Jimmy, who had grown up in the forests of Alger County. To the convict, the interrelationships between the island, its plants, and wildlife were fascinating. It was he who pointed out to Jimmy that except for the beaver there were no rodents on the island, and that plants were better hitchhikers than animals. Every species on the island had been transported from somewhere else and, once there, had been subjected to some genetic change, except for those beach species who constantly received new genetic influences from the mainland and were thus held stable.

He fits on this island, Jimmy thought. *Probably for the first time in his life he feels like he belongs. Now that he can read and write,* Jimmy mused, *if he ever discovers libraries, there'll be an explosion in that man's head that will carry him way beyond anyone I ever knew.*

He found himself almost liking the man. *Better escape from this island soon,* Jimmy reasoned, *or I'll never make it home.*

There was little chance. Burkey continued to keep the keys to the *Alyce* on his person; and since he never left the island, Jimmy had little time to work unobserved.

Now and then the boy eyed the canoe, but his captor kept that chained to the *Alyce's* deck and there was no opportunity to cut it loose. Besides that, canoes and Lake Superior didn't mix.

But the canoe trips up and down the island's waterways to count loons were safe enough, and a welcome diversion. Out on the lakes, the bugs let them alone, and every turn brought new vistas, new biotic communities. The canoe prowled gracefully and silently where a man could not have walked afoot without miring in the quaking bogs. The wolf pup stood front paws on the gunwales, missing nothing of what went on along shore. When mother scoters and black ducks rushed off, with babies pattering behind, toward the safety of shoreline grasses, the wolf went wild, and it was all Jimmy could do to keep him from leaping out of the canoe.

If the insect life on the island attracted birds and made humans miserable, it also made possible a diversity of carnivorous plants such as sundews, Venus's flytraps, and pitcher plants. Burkey's first introduction to the tiny sundew was to watch it clutch and devour a dragonfly twenty times its size; and when the man opened a Venus's flytrap, in the liquid that poured forth he found a collection representing most of the island's flying insects. Even Jimmy was impressed.

But however much Jimmy enjoyed prowling the forests or drifting across the lakes, land was not his passion. He longed for the feel of the *Alyce,* pitching and rolling through a real Lake Superior storm, the sting of wind-flung spray cold and wet upon his cheeks, the sight of green water crashing against the hull, or even the pull of a giant lake trout, emerging from mysterious depths at the end of his trolling line.

He was homesick too for the easy cameraderie of Munising where the sheriff knew every kid in town on a first-name basis, and cared. How many boys had he kept out of trouble with heart-to-heart talks? He missed Sunday dinner at the Brownstone Inn, where Diane, lovely and dark-eyed, served him up many a double portion to "help him grow"; and often as not, garbed in a pretty hostess gown, came over to sit with him while he ate, to the envy of grownup men in the room.

The *Alyce* sat there in the harbor like Banker Shipsey's trotting horse before the county fair, eager to be off. Her engine hadn't been started since freeze-up the fall before, and the big marsh spiders had built skeins of webs across the locked door of the cabin.

If only Burkey would be careless about the keys. But the man must realize that if Jimmy escaped the island, his own sojourn on the Island of the Loons would soon be over.

One afternoon, as Jimmy walked in the woods not far from the cabin, he flushed a mourning dove from her eggs on a platform of twigs and climbed a leaning windfall to peer inside. The young were almost ready to fly and regarded him with soft, liquid eyes. He backed carefully down the log, hoping not to frighten them into premature flight.

Breaking out in a sweat from exertion, he sat down on a mound of moss to rest. A wave of nausea swept over him, and he realized that this was something more than just an upset stomach. He was sick.

He remembered reading about a fever campers and trappers sometimes got from drinking water contaminated by beaver, but right now he could not recall more. He wished that he had been more careful where he drank, had been careful to slake his thirst only from the big lake.

No matter how often he wiped his brow on his sleeve, perspiration made his eyes smart. He stumbled on and had nearly gained the cabin when the world closed in on him. He saw the wolf pup running toward him, expecting to play, then everything went black as he fell. He was vaguely aware that the pup was tugging on his pant leg, and he heard Burkey's voice calling from far away.

When he awoke, he was on the big bed in the

cabin, and his head pounded with pain. He was aware that the bedclothes were soaked with sweat and clammy. A subdued wolf pup lay with his nose on his paws and regarded him; and Burkey sat in his chair, head cradled in his big hands.

He gathered enough strength to talk, but his voice was thin, his lips dry as wood chips. "Hey," he said, "get back to your loons. I'm okay. Honest."

Relief showed on the big man's face. "To hell with the loons, Pard," Burkey said. "You've been out of it so long the young are big enough to fly." Beneath Burkey's beard Jimmy saw his lips curve in what might have been a smile.

The room faded again. He wished he could ask Burkey for some water. Pure water this time. He remembered reading in school about the bug one could catch from beaver. *Giardia* something. *Giardia lamblia.* He had missed the name in a biology test, but he remembered it now. Lord knew what other bugs flourished in that organic soup on the island. His mouth and throat were parched as an old pair of leather boots. He felt suddenly cold.

He was at the bottom of the Munising Trench trying to swim upward through the frigid green depths. He saw a tall sandy-haired man holding out a hand to him. He'd seen the man before—on the beach once at Munising, looking out of place in Oxfords, and once he had caught him on the dock, standing alone, looking at the *Alyce.* He tried to reach out for the man's hand, but hands and feet seemed disconnected with his brain, refusing orders. "I know you! You're my father!"

"Hang in there, Jimmy!" Burkey's voice. The man faded.

"Jimmy!" It was the first time Burkey had called him by name!

twenty one

FOR DAYS, BURKEY SCARCELY left the boy's side. With the same singleminded intensity with which he had learned to read and to write, carve wildlife from wood, or study the life history of loons, he nursed the boy he held captive.

Even the wolf haunted the cabin, tail held low, caudal spot tight to his rump, as though he sensed the convict's sadness and concern. Now and then as Burkey rose to put a new log on the fire, he turned back to see the pup standing front feet on the bed, moist black nose against the boy's hot cheek. At other times he lay watching, dark-eyed and alert, seeking a corner as far away from the stove as possible, his nose to the cooler air along the floor.

Once it seemed that the boy would recover from the fever, but pneumonia set in, and Jimmy had to struggle hard for breath. Had his patient not been so helpless, Burkey might have opted for a quick trip to Canada for medicine; but the young life hung in such precarious balance, the man could not leave his side.

Desperate, Burkey went off into the woods and came back with armloads of plants and roots. He had no idea which of them might have medicinal qualities, but he had to try. And so he boiled them all. Great clouds of steam from the pots and buckets turned the cabin into a sauna. The wolf slipped out the door and sought the top of the ridge where a breeze off Lake Superior fanned the growing ruff along his neck.

Jimmy drifted into delirium. He was back at the Brownstone Inn, asking for Diane; but the stranger who waited on him had never heard of her. His friend, Mrs. Derleth, clad in a white apron, came out of the kitchen. Tears streamed down her cheeks, and on a tray, she held a little mound of smoking charcoal. "Oh, dear, Jimmy," she complained. "This is what always happens when I try to bake on Wednesday instead of Thursday."

Jimmy's mother swept into the dining room, black hair showing a touch of gray. Behind her paraded Jimmy's three red-maned sisters. He introduced his family to the other diners. "This is Alyce," he said. "And Alyce, and Alyce, and Alyce."

He drifted away and was suddenly on the pier looking down at the other *Alyce,* his fishing tug, newly painted and gleaming with chrome. Honest Risku, the sheriff was there.

"Hey, Jimmy," he said. "You look pretty pert fo' a guy that's dead!"

132

A tourist lady asked Honest to take her photograph with her family. Honest took the camera, stepped back to get them in the viewer, and fell off the dock into Lake Superior. In his delirium, Jimmy laughed so hard he began to choke, and Riggs Burkey rushed to his side. For a moment it was as though the boy had died, then, gradually, his breathing came back quiet and even, and he slept.

When he awoke, Burkey was gone, and the cabin seemed unbearably hot. The wolf trotted in the open door and leaped to the bed, towering over the boy. Jimmy shrank back from him. It was not the pup he remembered.

Burkey came in the door carrying a pail of blue-berries and set it on the table.

"What happened to the pup?" Jimmy asked. "This guy's huge."

Burkey looked first at Jimmy, then at the wolf. He burst into a laugh Jimmy had never heard before. "You been out of it for weeks, Jimmy, and all that pup had to do was lay around and eat." He came over to the bed and looked down at the boy. "How you feel?" He did not wait for an answer.

"You've been a case," the big man grumbled, as though embarrassed by his tenderness. "Like to talked my ear off. Never had a cellmate bad as you. Expect I met half the folks in Munising."

He went over to the stove and dipped up a cup of broth, wiped it off, and brought it to the bed. "Here," he said, "drink this. Put a little meat on your bones."

Reaching for the cup, Jimmy paused midway to

look at his body in astonishment. The hand was so thin and the arm so white it couldn't be his. In the end, Burkey had to hold the cup to his lips so he could drink. The broth felt good on his parched lips. He drank it slowly, then lay back to rest while Burkey brought him more.

Four days later, Burkey picked him up like a rag doll and set him out on a blanket in the midst of a patch of blueberries. Jimmy looked about in wonder, peering through his fingers to accustom his eyes to the glare.

There were no mosquitoes left, and the lady slippers that had covered the floor of the forest in pink profusion were gone, replaced by an azure carpet of blueberries. He picked a handful and filled his mouth, marveling at their sweetness. In the forest, a northern waterthrush was paying final homage to summer, and far off he could hear a flight of loons. In the harbor below, he could see the *Alyce* still nodding gently on those few swells that managed to round the cliff from the big lake.

A few days later, he made his first walk about the island. Burkey went along, and together, as the wolf hunted the thickets, they explored for new plants, pondering over their discoveries, trying to guess what they might be. "There must be books out," Burkey guessed. "Books that'd give names to every plant in the world. Sure wish I had some!"

He waded out into a bog and emerged, dripping but triumphant. "We're going to call this 'Sundew Bog,'" he crowed! "Look here! Four different kinds of sundews. And look at this," he said, holding up a handful of moss. "One of these little plants is so mean it's trying to eat my finger. See, it's already reddened the skin!"

As they crossed an ester through a forest of birch and mountain ash, they paused to eat their fill of highbush huckleberries and stuffed their pockets with dandelion greens and miner's lettuce for supper. A family of loons flew overhead, calling loudly. Already the young were flying with their parents, heading out to feed on the big lake.

Burkey watched them until they disappeared over the trees. His exuberance of the moment before vanished; he seemed sad, as though realizing that soon it would be autumn, and the loons would leave him for warmer climes.

The man was often sad of late. Gone was the surly, brutal convict of old. But still he seemed to struggle with his sensitivities, not quite ready to give in, uncomfortable with a new self. Often Jimmy awoke late at night to find Burkey still sitting beside the lamp at the table, writing letters; but when he finished them, he crumpled them in his huge fist and watched them burn to a nothingness of gray ash in the stove. He seemed to cling to every day as though it were his last, cherishing each trailing afterglow of daylight. It was pitch dark before he would come into the cabin.

One evening, as he sat writing in the puddle of the old lamp's yellow light, he finished a letter and sat quietly reading it, tracing every word with his forefinger as though carefully weighing its meaning. Instead of destroying it, he folded it carefully and placed it in the pocket of his shirt. When Jimmy opened his eyes again, Burkey still sat at the table, but asleep, his shaggy head resting on his arms.

At dawn he left the cabin without breakfast, and glancing down from the cabin, Jimmy saw him cross over the gangway planks to the *Alyce*.

Now and then as Jimmy made himself breakfast, he heard pounding, and once Burkey emerged from the cabin to the afterdeck, a big wrench in his hand. Soon the engine pounded into life, and rings of blue smoke drove high into the trees until they were swept away by the prevailing winds.

"Going someplace in her?" Jimmy asked as the man returned to the cabin. Burkey only glanced at him and turned away without answering; and Jimmy let the matter drop.

During the night, Jimmy awoke to see that Burkey still sat at the table, working away at a loon carving, polishing it with love. In the morning the man was gone. Alarmed, Jimmy rushed to the cabin door. The *Alyce* still bobbed in the harbor, but man and wolf had disappeared. On the table, anchored down by the keys to the *Alyce*, were two letters in Burkey's handwriting.

The first note was addressed to him. It read:

Friend Jimmy
All my life I've been a loon in another loon's territory. On this island I found my place on

Earth; someday I hope to return to live out my life here.

I reckon the wildlife here needs someone to go to bat for it, especially the loons, but before I can help I've got to fill some real holes in my education. With the right books, maybe, I could do that here, but I've got to settle some accounts.

I was wrong to keep you here on this land, but when a man's freedom is at stake, he sometimes does desperate things.

Here are the keys to your boat. Please give the other note to the sheriff in Munising. It should interest him.

I'd go with you but I need a few days on the island to make sure the wolf can hunt for himself. I am enclosing some cash in an envelope addressed to a church in Marquette. I want them to have a door for their rectory far better than the one I stole. As I am able to sell carvings, I hope to pay back everything I've taken. The loon carving is yours to remember me by.

The wolf and I are going to the north end of the island, which will give you time to take the *Alyce* and go. Write sometimes, Jimmy, and let me know how things are with you.

Sincerely,
Riggs Burkey

The other note was to prison authorities.

To Whom It May Concern:

I am alive on an island in Lake Superior, N.E. Caribou Light. Camped on S.E. end where island drainage enters Lake Superior.

I wish to settle my business with the state. You can come unarmed. I do not wish to harm anyone.

Signed,
Riggs Burkey
#390507

twenty two

JIMMY TOOK THE NOTES, the money, and the carving of the loon and sauntered down to the *Alyce,* savoring a delicious feeling of being free. Why hurry and spoil the moment? The engine started first try, as though the *Alyce* were anxious to be off. As the engine idled, warming up, he winched the rusty anchor up on the deck, brushing off an accumulation of snails. Moments later, the *Alyce* eased around the corner of the cliff, and the cabin was lost to view.

A stiff wind was blowing from the northeast, a homeward wind. Excitement buoyed in him as he headed carefully out past the reefs, moving slowly, painstakingly cautious so as not to ruin his journey to freedom.

As he passed the last reef and turned southward into open seas, he pictured headlines as they might appear in the *Munising News.*

LOCAL BOY RETURNS FROM DEAD

Held prisoner on a deserted island in Lake Superior by an escaped convict, Jimmy Munising, long considered drowned, sailed his fishing tug, *Alyce,* into Munising Harbor, bearing a note from the convict that he wished to turn himself in. Authorities are en route to the island by helicopter to return the man, Riggs Burkey, to the prison in Marquette.

He could see his picture on the front page, with Diane planting a kiss on his cheek. But then he thought of Burkey, alone now on his Island of the Loons, and a sadness came over him. In his mind's eye, he saw himself putting out of Munising Harbor loaded with staples that would help Burkey become the scientist he wanted to be. Books, microscope, supplies. His anger, after all, was with a man who no longer existed. The new Burkey had expressed a desire to pay back what he had once stolen, and the contribution he might make on that island—wasn't that sacrifice enough, an atonement for past misdeeds?

Only he knew Riggs Burkey was still alive, and it would be easy enough to come up with a story about where he and the *Alyce* had been. Off to Duluth or some other metropolis along the western shore. Off sowing his oats like a lot of other homeless kids his age.

Time and again as he beat toward the Michigan shore, he changed his mind. He passed a sleek sport trawler out after coho, and the skipper eyed the clumsy old *Alyce* curiously and perhaps wondered why she dared the lake so far from shore. Outside of Riggs Burkey, this was the first human he had seen since the ore boat had gone down over a year before.

Far off, he could see the blue outline of the old familiar hills surrounding Munising harbor, and the buckskin mirage of a distant sandy beach. There would be people along that beach, some of them friends, but most of them tourists. Jimmy felt suddenly shy.

The water surrounding the *Alyce* was a deep blue; they were over the Munising Trench, the deepest part of Lake Superior. The Island of the Loons already seemed like a half-forgotten dream, as unreal as the hallucinations he'd had when he was sick in the cabin, and Riggs Burkey sat caring for him.

Jimmy eased off on the throttle, leaned his arms across the top of the wheel, and buried his face in agony. It was awful, that irony. If Burkey had not saved his life, he would not now be heading in to turn him over to the authorities.

Letting the *Alyce* steer her own course, he moved to the aft rail and watched the tug's wake. He held Burkey's letters outstretched in his hand; one slip and they would be gone forver. He laid the papers on the railing, hoping the wind would make the decision for him, but the letters rode the railing as though nailed down. Putting them back in his pocket, he returned to the wheel.

No one recognized the *Alyce* as she chugged into her old moorings. The cabin had been repainted, and there was no longer a name embossed on her sides. The boy glanced shyly at the faces along the dock. Not a soul there he'd seen before. Maybe, like Rip Van Winkle, he'd been asleep for years, and all his friends were dead and gone. In that case he could burn Burkey's letters.

He could see old familiar buildings. Everything seemed as he had left it, including Horus Matson's old store. Then, suddenly, as he was making the *Alyce* fast to her moorings, he saw Honest Risku driving down in his patrol car as though to check out the new arrival.

The sheriff parked and strolled over to where a tourist was having trouble with an ice machine. It was reassuring: the same old Honest, looking not a day older than before.

The sheriff's glance swept over Jimmy and moved on. If his eyes narrowed, it was perhaps because he took Jimmy with his ragged clothes and long red hair as merely another transient beach bum to be carefully watched.

"Sheriff Risku!" Jimmy called. "Hey! Wait up! It's me! Jimmy Munising!"

The sheriff whirled in his tracks, pale as though he'd just seen a ghost. "Jimmy! My God! It's Jimmy, sure enough." He rushed to the boy and caught him up in a bear hug. "It's Jimmy Munising!" he exclaimed to the tourists on the dock as though they should all have recognized him.

"Where the hell you been, Boy?"

Jimmy's heart sank. This was the moment he had

been dreading. Hands trembling, he fished in his pocket and handed over Riggs Burkey's note.

As if by magic, word of his arrival spread through the town. Windows opened, faces peered out as though expecting him to parade before their houses. Switchboards jammed. Church bells rang. Newcomers who had never heard of Jimmy thronged beside natives, all moving toward the docks. And, of course, someone thought to telephone Alyce Marie, Alyce Ruth, and Alyce Anne to let them know their brother Jimmy was arrived back from the dead.

Jimmy watched the sheriff's face as he read Riggs Burkey's note.

"Sheriff Risku," Jimmy said. "You suppose you could do me a favor? I want you to keep that letter under your hat for right now and go out yourself and bring him in. Just special for me. You see, turning himself in was his idea not mine. He's my friend, Sheriff, and that sort of makes him your friend, too."

For a moment the sheriff paled at the thought of heading out to a remote island in Lake Superior all alone to bring in an escaped convict. Once again he read Burkey's words and seemed to feel better.

"OK, Jimmy," he agreed. "Just for you."

Buttoning the letter carefully in his shirt pocket, he set out to fuel his launch for the trip. He was feeling happier all the time. After all, bringing in Riggs Burkey, all alone, would be the biggest adventure of his career.

twenty three

JIMMY'S RETICENCE ABOUT WHERE he had been left the people of Munising suspecting that there was a good deal more to his story than met the eye; but they were so glad to have him back that to his face at least they respected his privacy.

Behind his back, however, speculation ran rife; and the story that took precedence over others was that he had located his natural father, a redhaired millionaire lawyer from Duluth, who had tried to subject the boy to concerts and country clubs; but the boy had rebelled, let his hair grow long in defiance, and come home to Munising and his true friends.

When four days had passed and still Honest Risku had not returned, Jimmy began to worry first that Honest had run afoul of the reefs, then, that Riggs Burkey had not really reformed. *If anything happens to poor old Honest,* Jimmy thought, *I'll be responsible. Maybe I was a fool to send him out alone.* In his mind,

144

a troublesome picture kept forming of the sheriff's big patrol launch, Burkey alone at the wheel, scooting away from the Island of the Loons, bound for parts unknown.

He was vastly relieved, one afternoon, to see the patrol boat speed up to the Munising docks with the sheriff and Burkey aboard. Jimmy thought the men looked more like fishing buddies than a sheriff bringing in a criminal. Burkey, Jimmy soon discovered, had asked the sheriff for another day to pack and say good-bye to the island. By the time that day had passed, Honest had fallen under the island's spell and was so impressed with Burkey's feel for Nature, that he himself had suggested another couple of days.

"He's got ideas," Honest told Jimmy. "Ideas for a wildlife refuge on that island you wouldn't believe. It's a shame . . ." His excitement faded as he thought to himself that some judge or another might put a swift end to Burkey's dreams.

A few idlers, noting that the sheriff's boat had arrived with a passenger, began to gather. Quickly, Jimmy and the two men tied up the launch, climbed into the patrol car, and moments later were speeding up the highway to the Brownstone Inn. "Man takes a prisoner, he's got to feed him." Honest grinned. "Hope you can stand whitefish one more time."

Sitting on her apprehensions, the fair Diane locked and bolted the dining room doors to the public so that she could better accommodate her friends. It was only a matter of minutes before she had whipped them up a whitefish dinner fit for a king.

As though astonished that such food existed, **Riggs Burkey** pitched in and ate as though there were no tomorrow. Midway through the meal, however, he glanced up to notice that Jimmy and Honest were only picking at their food.

"Hey," he said. "What's wrong?"

"I'm not hungry," Jimmy said.

"Me neither," Honest put in, cupping his chin in one huge hand, mouth turned down at the corners. "Once we drive up to that prison with Riggs, things will happen in a hurry. Reporters, photographers—the whole bit. Nobody will believe Riggs turned himself in, and I'll end up a hero of sorts. But believe you me, I don't like being a part of all this."

"Way I see it," Jimmy said, "Riggs Burkey is dead. I mean, you're not the same guy you were when you—well, when you invited me to stay on the island. You'd be taking punishment for a guy who no longer exists. And besides, once you're locked up, there won't be anyone to worry about the loons."

"Jimmy's right," Honest put in, brightening considerably. "That convict is dead. You say otherwise, but look at the facts. Burkey couldn't read or write. You can. Burkey wouldn't have nursed Jimmy back to life. You did." He grinned at the man. "Way I see it, you're just another of those psychos who get a compulsion to admit to crimes they didn't commit."

Riggs Burkey smiled at his friends. "It's no use, you guys," he said. "I am a different person now, and the guy I happen to feel like is somebody ready to take what's coming to him. I can use the time to work at carving birds and pay back every penny I've ever stolen."

"But they'll throw away the key," Honest protested.

"Maybe," Burkey admitted. "But maybe not. Right now prisons are full to bursting. I'd served most of my sentence when I walked away, and I'm willing to gamble that the judge who sentences me for escaping and the stealing I did will treat me fair. The next time I walk away from prison, I want it to be as a free man."

All this time Diane had been busy about the room, but she hadn't missed a word. When she came over with a tray of desserts, her cheeks were shiny with tears. "Must be an allergy," she apologized, wiping her face with a napkin. "Goldenrod. Never could stand to be around it."

"I've got an idea," Jimmy said, holding a chair for Diane. "We drive Riggs back to the prison farm; he sneaks back over the fence and joins the other prisoners. He'll get credit for turning himself in, and Honest and I will be spared telling a pack of lies because nobody will guess we're involved. I can see it now; the guard makes a head count, comes up with one too many, and finds out he's got a walkback. I like it!"

The sheriff and Burkey were still mulling over Jimmy's plan when a knock sounded on the restaurant door.

Diane turned pale and struggled up from her seat.

"We're closed," she said. "Try us again tomorrow."

"State Police, ma'am. We saw the sheriff's car parked outside, found the door locked, and thought we'd check that everything is all right."

"Let them in," Burkey said, and Diane unbolted the door.

"Come in and have coffee, folks!" she said at her gracious best.

The two patrolmen entered the room, their glances sweeping the group at the table.

"Everything's under control," Honest Risku said. "But thanks for checking it out."

"No sweat, Honest," one of the officers said. He glanced at Diane, who was taking a couple of mugs from the shelf behind the counter.

"No coffee, Ma'am. If you don't mind we'll be on our way."

The two men had turned toward the door to go when Burkey rose slowly to his feet.

"Gentlemen," he said. "Let me introduce myself. My name is Riggs Burkey, an escaped convict come back from the dead. Sheriff Risku here is on his way to the prison in Marquette to turn me in."

twenty four

ONCE AGAIN WORD SPREAD FAST. When Jimmy and Honest arrived back in Munising, from helping take Riggs Burkey to Marquette, a large crowd had assembled to wait for them at city hall. Jimmy slipped from the sheriff's patrol car and tried to amble off as though nothing had happened.

"There he goes!" someone shouted, and the crowd flowed around him, pressing close. A reporter from the *News* staked out rights to the story by clipping the microphone from his tape recorder to Jimmy's jacket front.

"What'll I say, Honest?" Jimmy whispered, wishing he were back on the *Alyce.*

"I guess now it'd help Riggs most if you told everything, Jim," the sheriff answered. He took charge of the crowd. "Now, folks, this here boy has a story to tell. Push back away there and give him air!"

Jimmy began his story, aware that what he left

out the reporter would drag out of him. He told of seeing the ore boat go down, saving the convict, building the cabin, trying to escape. He told of Burkey's broken leg, the man's singleminded determination to learn to read by studying a bird guide. He waxed eloquent about subsequent changes in the convict's character, told how Burkey had devoted his days to studying loons and, last but not least, had saved his life through tender devoted care. Little by little, Riggs Burkey began to emerge as some sort of folk hero.

"And now," Jimmy said, making one last final pitch for his friend, "this man who could have lived out his days, dead and forgotten on the island, chose to send me back to civilization and turn himself in so that he might pay his debts to society and return to the island and devote his life to the loons."

Quietly, Jimmy unhooked the microphone and handed it back to the reporter. He had put the crowd in the position of being judge and jury, and left them silent. As they pondered the events, they hardly seemed to noticed the boy as he walked through them and sought refuge in the old store nearby.

The prison authorities in Marquette were quick to realize that they had more than a simple walk-back on their hands. When the President of National Audubon Society, and the International Director of the Nature Conservancy both visited the prison to talk to Riggs Burkey about the wisdom of a fund-raising to establish the Island of the Loons as a refuge for endangered loons and rare plants, and held out hope they might fund his future studies, the administration refused to comment; but everyone involved privately pondered Riggs' case. As a public hero, Riggs Burkey could become a real problem.

It must be said of the prosecution that they were eminently fair. In light of all the publicity, and with the support of the governor himself, they sent down state for one of their most respected hearings officers, Judge Hiram D. McComber, who had the reputation for being tough but fair, and gave him the task of researching the case and sentencing the prisoner.

On the day of reckoning, the courtroom was so packed with media representatives that Jimmy and his three sisters, who had joined him for the ordeal, had little choice but to stand in the rear. Jimmy waved encouragement to Burkey when he was brought in and was a little upset that Burkey looked downright sad and discouraged. The girls kept looking up at their brother as though in awe of what he had gotten himself into.

Called as a witness at last, Jimmy identified Riggs Burkey as the man who had survived the sinking of the *Charles H. Schaffer* and told his story simply and well, as might have been expected with all the practice he had gained of late.

Veterans of Judge McComber's court noted that the judge had a little trouble looking at the boy, but lay back in his chair staring at the ceiling, and only once interrupted, and that was to ask the boy to repeat his name. When Jimmy replied "Jimmy Munising," the judge seemed for the moment mollified. The pre-sentencing investigation, after all, had turned up that Jimmy's mother had died a few years back and that Jimmy was a ward of the town.

"Unusual! Most unusual!" the judge commented at Jimmy's story; but the fact that Jimmy, at the age of fourteen, had practically owned his own fishing tug seemed to meet with Judge McComber's approval and lend credibility to his story.

Local betting, however, had it that old "Hard Nose Hiram" would give Burkey so many years he would be too old when he got out to study loons. Angry mutterings of dissension were already rampant in the community and had been echoed in the press.

Since Burkey had admitted his guilt, the hearing sped to its finish; and in due course, Burkey was thrust before the judge for sentencing. A murmur of excitement ran through the courtroom; and, in an atmosphere of anticipation, Jimmy's three sisters crowded as a body down the aisle to the front of the courtroom to be with their brother at this trying moment.

Judge Hiram McComber stared first at the girls with their flowing red tresses, then at Jimmy with his carrot top.

"What's your name?" the Judge asked, forgetting the defendant, and looking down at the first sister.

"Alyce Marie, Sir."

"And yours?"

"Alyce Ruth."

"And yours?"

"Alyce Anne. We're Jimmy's sisters, Sir, but our last name is Hiram. At least that's the name our mother used. Her name was Alyce, too."

The judge covered his eyes for a moment and shook his balding head. An assistant, thinking that the judge might be ill, moved toward him, but he motioned him away.

"Young Man!" the judge said, looking hard at Jimmy. "You're the injured party in this case. At least the most prominent one. If you wore my robes, how would you pass sentence on this man?"

"Why, Sir," Jimmy replied, "I guess I'd throw the book at him. Several books in fact. I'd give him five years—"

There was a startled buzz about the courtroom, and Burkey looked down at the floor.

"Order in the court!" the judge cried. "Proceed, Mr. Munising."

"—five years probation with the understanding he use his talents to conduct a loon study on the island and serve as its guardian. You see, Sir, that island deserves protection. It's one of the last strongholds of loons in North America, as well as a resting place for other bird migrants trying to cross Lake Superior. With Riggs there to study and protect, with reference books to continue his education, why, Sir, society would end up owing him."

A gasp of relief ran through the audience; for the

first time, "Hard Nose Hiram" was seen to smile.

"Order in the court! The prisoner will stand for sentencing."

He looked down on Riggs Burkey. "Mr. Burkey," he said. "I can't speak for the Board of Paroles. They have the say on the time you had left to serve when you escaped. I would hope that due to crowded conditions in the prison, which currently have, in many cases, effected early release, they might be lenient. For my part," he went on, glancing at Jimmy and the girls, "I hereby sentence you to five years probation, during which time you will live on the island, fund yourself with your talents as a woodcarver, and devote every available moment to your study of loons. During that time you will do everything in your power to bring about in the public an appreciation of endangered species and work to see that the Island of the Loons becomes a wildlife sanctuary."

Riggs Burkey should have kept facing the judge, but it was hard for him to keep from turning. He looked first at Jimmy, thanks evident in his glance. Then he looked at Honest, whose grin seemed to flash like candles in a jack-o-lantern. For a long moment his eyes searched the crowd, as though looking in vain for someone who did not wish him well. At long last, he looked at Diane, tears of relief brimming in her eyes. She didn't know a loon from an albatross, at that point, but sensed it might be interesting to learn.

As to the press, who are generally so alert and

sensitive to stories, in practically trampling each other to get to telephones, not one of them noted something that may have had some significance. It was the sight of Judge Hiram D. McComber escorting Jimmy and his sisters into his private chambers.

AUTHOR'S NOTE

A few notes on *Island of the Loons*. The island actually exists some eighty miles from shore in eastern Lake Superior. Except for changing its name, and the appearance of the shoreline for its own protection, the island is close to being as described.

In 1982, I spent some time on the island making bird and plant surveys as part of a team of interested persons trying to save the island from development. Close to zero hour we were successful in placing the island in a conservation trust.

Hyde, Dayton O.

Island of the loons

$12.95